VANILLA BEAN VENGEANCE

CLAIRE'S CANDLES - BOOK 1

AGATHA FROST

INTRODUCTION FROM AGATHA FROST

Hello there! Agatha Frost here! I'm so excited to introduce you to my brand new series, Claire's Candles. The series follows candle-enthusiast and amateur thirty-five-year-old sleuth, Claire Harris, in the small (fictional) English village of Northash.

Some of you may know me from my bestselling Peridale Cafe series, but if not, no need to worry because this is a fully standalone series! If you're new to my books, I hope you enjoy this outing, and if you're a regular reader of my work, thank you for the support over the past three years!

If you're new to my work, I'd like to point out that, being a British author who writes British mysteries, my books are written in British English, so some spellings and phrases might be a little different than you're used to, but isn't that the fun of reading?

I hope you enjoy meeting Claire and the rest of the Northash residents in their first outing! It's been a lot of fun crafting this new world for you, so I hope you enjoy the results.

Claire's Candles Cozy Mystery Series

Vanilla Bean Vengeance

Agatha Frost

CHAPTER ONE

*T*he small shop was perfect. Claire Harris walked around the empty space, her heart fluttering with excitement. She knew exactly how she would decorate it, how she would arrange the displays. How could she not? She'd spent years daydreaming about owning her very own candle shop.

"I'd put the counter right here," she said, standing where she would spend her days and looking out the single-paned bay window onto the village square. The spring daylight streamed into the shop in dusty golden lines. "And the seasonal candles right here."

"It's the perfect size," said Sally Halliwell, the estate agent. "Places like this don't come up often."

"I know."

Claire had spent years waiting for the perfect shop,

but things rarely changed in the small Lancashire village of Northash. Jane's Tearoom had only closed because Jane's daughter, happy being a yoga instructor, hadn't wanted to take over the family business. Jane clung on for as long as she could, more for the sake of her regulars than anything else. Single-handedly running a café wasn't as easy fifteen years past retirement, according to Jane's emotional speech on closing day.

"I'd make the candles in here." Claire walked through to the kitchen at the back. "It's compact, but perfect for what I need. Small runs of artisan candles, made in Northash, sold in Northash. Nobody is doing it."

"I can smell them now."

"And the flat upstairs!" Claire spun around, clinging to the doorframe. "I'd only have to come down a single flight of stairs to work."

"The dream."

"I could wake up ten minutes before opening."

"Would you like to see the flat again?"

Claire nodded, beaming from ear to ear.

Sally led the way through the side door in the kitchen, up the narrow staircase, and into the living quarters above. The flat was made up of an open-plan kitchen, living, and dining area, with two small bedrooms and a bathroom. The roof sloped at the front and the back, but Claire was short enough that her head was well shy of grazing the ceiling. It was dated and small by anyone's standards, but so were most places in Northash. For Claire, it beat living with her parents.

"South-facing front windows," Sally explained, consulting the brochure. "No damp, good attic insulation, and the gas safety certificate is up to date. A lick of paint and a new carpet would drag it into 2020."

The floral wallpaper wasn't to Claire's tastes, but somehow, for the sake of her dream, she didn't mind it. She had never visited when it was Jane's flat, but she could easily imagine the inevitable high-backed velvet chairs, porcelain ornaments, and lace doilies. Like most everyone else in town, she still couldn't believe quiet and meek Jane Brindle had left Northash for a new life in France.

"Big enough for one," Claire said almost to herself as she walked over to the front window. "And pets are allowed."

"Rare around here."

Claire looked through the small window, and it felt strange to be seeing the village square from up above. Beyond the small clock tower in the middle of the square stood The Hesketh Arms pub, doubtless already filled with people having a pint and pie on their lunch breaks. Similar-sized shops with similar flats above lined the rest of the square, all quietly busy, keeping the village's small economy ticking. Northash, at least, was still valiantly fending off corporate invasion in favour of small local businesses.

"I'll take it."

Claire spun around, and for a brief moment, she and Sally stared at each other with the same pursed lips. The laughter broke free, bursting Claire's fantasy with it.

Sally joined her at the window, and they looked out together. Mrs Beaton, one of Claire's elderly neighbours at the cul-de-sac, was out with one of her many reluctant cats fastened into a pink harness, picking up the odd bits of rubbish and putting them in the bins. Sally rested a hand on Claire's shoulder, the weight of reality behind it.

"It won't stay on the market forever," Sally said softly, her professional tone gone. "We've had a bit of interest already."

"I know."

"Can you still not afford it?"

Claire pulled her phone from her pocket and opened up her banking app. Using her thumbprint as the password, she revealed the £456.89 in her current account and the £2.34 in savings. She didn't mind showing Sally. They'd been close friends since their school days.

"Not even enough for the deposit and first month's rent." Claire slotted the phone back into her pocket. "Can barely get shifts at the factory since Nicola brought in the zero-hours contracts."

"You know your—"

"Parents would lend me the money?" Claire interjected. "I know, I know. But it's not their dream, it's mine."

"Your dad would give it to you in a heartbeat."

"I couldn't ask him."

"Well, if you don't want to be stuck working at the candle factory for the rest of your life, you need to act sooner rather than later." Sally squeezed Claire's shoulder a final time before pulling away. "Right, I need to get back to work. Got a couple of viewings over in Skipton."

"*Real* viewings, you mean."

"I didn't say that."

"I know." Claire smiled. "Thanks for showing it to me again."

They were on their third viewing, and Claire was no closer to being able to afford it. She had hoped glimpsing her dream again would have inspired the money in her bank account to grow; it had not.

"You make the *best* candles," Sally said as they descended the narrow staircase. "Even my mother-in-law loved that new vanilla one you gave me, and she doesn't like *anything*."

Claire had spent weeks perfecting her latest vanilla creation. People always assumed it was as simple as throwing vanilla extract into wax, but Claire knew differently. Base notes of vanilla, middle notes of caramel and white musk, and a top note of sugar had resulted in Claire's best vanilla candle yet. Simple, yet sweet and seductive, and powerful enough to fill an entire room as soon as the lid was taken off, all without being cloying. She appreciated the praise, but scents were one of the few things she knew she was good at without needing validation. Her nose did the work for her.

"We'll have dinner soon, okay?" Sally locked the front door. "Paul is still working his behind off for that promotion, and the kids are driving me up the wall now they're on Easter break. Who knew adulthood would be so stressful, eh? I could use a girl's night out."

They hugged before Sally climbed into her car. Claire lingered outside the shop, waving Sally off. As she watched the car leave the village square, she knew Sally's girl's night out was as much a fantasy as Claire's dream of opening a shop.

At thirty-five, they were the same age, but their lives couldn't have worked out more differently. Claire and Sally had attended school together, inseparable through it all. Best friends for life – and they had the matching necklaces to prove it. Sally stopped wearing hers in their early twenties, but she insisted she had it in a drawer somewhere. Claire hadn't seen it in years. Claire kept her necklace in her jewellery box; it meant more to her than it did to Sally.

Sally provided a glimpse into an alternate reality

where the focus was climbing the career ladder and being a wife and mother. Sally had always dreamed of having a family, and she had it.

Claire had only ever dreamed of the candle shop.

The shop was just as perfect from the outside looking in, even with the lights off. Claire didn't resent Sally for her life. She was truly happy for her oldest friend. It wasn't Sally's fault Claire had spent the past seventeen years working on the assembly line in the candle factory. A job close enough to her dream to get her out of bed in the morning, but low-paying enough to keep her real dream always just out of reach.

Pulling herself away from the shop and her dream, she crossed the square, smiling and waving at Mrs Beaton as she went. The old woman squinted through her saucer bifocals, waving back but not seeming to recognise Claire at all. Nobody knew Mrs Beaton's first name. Nobody knew Mrs Beaton's age. Nobody knew how many cats Mrs Beaton actually shared her home with. All Claire knew was that Mrs Beaton had lived in the same cul-de-sac as her parents longer than anyone could remember and had been an old woman for all that time.

Claire climbed the two steps into Marley's Café, the only option for a cup of tea and a slice of cake since Jane's Tearoom closed its doors for the final time. Marley's vegan café had always struggled to fill all its seats on any given day, even though it was smaller than Jane's place. Clearly, he no longer had this problem.

"Sorry I'm late." Claire kissed her father, Alan Harris, on the cheek and sat across from him, the café bustling with life around her. "Lost track of time."

Claire's father was her favourite person in the whole world, and she didn't mind admitting it to anyone who asked. She didn't make a habit of lying to him, but she hadn't told him about her fantasy viewings of the empty shop. She wouldn't have even told Sally if she hadn't been the estate agent, though she doubted she would have gone to see it at all if she weren't.

Maybe she should have stuck to staring through the window like she had for a month before plucking up the courage to ask for a look inside.

"It's all right, love." Alan rested his pen on the paper, the crossword half filled in. "Was just training my brain. Your mother says I've gone slow since I retired."

"You only retired last year."

"Try telling her that." He winked. "Forty years in the police force, twenty of those a detective, and she thinks my brain has turned to mush after a year of pottering around the garden." He glanced down at the paper, scratching the side of his bald head. "She might be onto something. Can't for the life of me figure this one out."

"Go on."

"Eight across, seven letters." He peered over his glasses. "Derogatory word for non-country dwellers."

"Townies."

From her angle, Claire saw the 'i' in 'zinc' crossed at the correct place; her father grinned and jotted it down.

"*Townies!*" He dropped the pen again. "You always were a clever girl."

"Tell that to my teachers at school."

"Exams mean nothing. You have a brain, and you know how to use it."

"I wish my brain could figure out a way to make more money."

"Whatever for?"

"Doesn't matter." She looked down at the chocolate brownie on his plate. "Mum would do a backflip if she knew you'd ordered a brownie."

He grinned and pushed the plate across to her. "This one is for you. I already had mine."

Claire bit into the brownie, so creamy and chocolatey she never would have guessed half its ingredients were substituted. Like most of the villagers, she'd always favoured Jane's Tearoom and had never given the vegan café much of a chance. Still, as much as she had liked Jane's traditional baking, she wasn't too proud to admit she preferred everything she'd tried of Marley's so far, vegan or not.

"I won't tell if you don't," she mumbled through the

mouthful. "Diets are boring anyway. And it's vegan. That must mean it's healthy, right?"

"Nothing tasting that good could ever be healthy."

"A moment on the lips, a lifetime on the hips."

"Now you sound like your mother."

Janet, her mother, had been trying to put Claire on a diet ever since she had been forced to move back in with them. Her mother was a tall and slender woman by nature, and she didn't seem to understand why Claire didn't look like her. Claire had inherited her father's body. Round and short, with the thin mousy hair and lousy eyesight to match. An apple shape on two stilts, she had always called it. She'd given up the dream of wanting to look like everyone else a long time ago. Only her mother still seemed to care.

As she finished the brownie, her father got back to his crossword. She looked around the café at the same faces she had been seeing her whole life. A couple smiled; she smiled back. Over her shoulder, the empty tearoom taunted her, and for the first time in her life, she wished she could give up that dream as quickly as she had every diet she had ever tried.

She was stuck, and she didn't know how to unstick herself.

CHAPTER TWO

*C*laire panicked the second her eyes opened the next morning. Without even having to look at the clock, she knew she was late for work. She'd gone to bed far too late to feel so well-rested.

She rolled over and the sun blinded her through a crack in the heavy blackout curtains. More evidence: it was too bright to be as early in the morning as she needed it to be.

After a dragged-out minute of denial, she pushed herself up and slapped her phone.

10:34 am.

Her shift started at 9 am.

A younger Claire might have sprung out of bed and run straight for the door, but she'd worked at the factory long enough to know she'd only get a verbal warning, and she rarely even got those.

She slammed her head back into her pillow, her mind fully awake. Phone in hand, she checked her alarms. Last night, she'd asked Siri to set the alarm for 8, but Siri had seen fit to set it for 8 pm and not 8 am.

Just my luck, she thought.

Her two precious cats, Sid and Domino, were curled up next to each other on the other side of the double bed, their contrasting colours making an almost perfect yin and yang symbol.

Sid, the fluffy ball of black fur, had come to her by accident three years ago. Claire had never suspected she was a cat person until Sally got Sid as a small black kitten and quickly realised both her young children were allergic. Claire had begrudgingly taken Sid in to avoid him going to the animal shelter. She had fallen in love before the end of their first day together.

Domino came a year later, this time on purpose. Sid went through a phase of scratching the wallpaper, and after asking around, she concluded he might be bored and lonely when she was working her long shifts at the factory. A quick trip to the local animal rescue resulted in bringing home a tiny stray kitten, white with little black patches. She had barely grown since. Claire and Sid fell in love with Domino before the end of their first afternoon together.

Once upon a time, they'd have woken her up long before the alarm, but their personalities had softened since they'd all been forced to leave their two-bedroom terraced workman's cottage on the other side of the village. Claire's landlord returning to Northash and needing his house back had been a blessing in disguise; with her new work hours, she'd never have been able to afford the rent.

Even though Sid and Domino had a giant four-bedroom detached cottage with a never-ending garden to explore, most days they confined themselves to the bedroom. Unlike Sally's kids, Claire's mother wasn't allergic to cats, but it didn't stop her from claiming she was. She'd only had to chase them away a couple of times for them to learn to keep their distance.

After giving them a little attention each, Claire forced herself out of bed, grateful she'd had a shower at 1 am. She'd hoped it would help her sleep after staying up all night, tossing and turning and thinking about the shop, but she'd still been awake late enough to see the clock get close to 3 am.

She dressed quickly in a blue jumpsuit, the standard uniform for the Warton Candle Factory. It did nothing for her figure, but then, it did nothing for anyone's figure. They all looked like blue Oompa Loompa's without the fun of bursting into song and dance every five minutes.

After flinging the curtains open, she fed the cats and

cleaned up what they'd left her in the litter tray overnight. As she left the room, she passed by the dressing table, which had become a makeshift candle-making station. She'd borrowed the equipment from work. Technically, she'd stolen it, though she'd heard on good authority it was being thrown out to be replaced anyway. Her mother thought she was insane bringing her work home with her, but Claire couldn't be creative and make the candles she wanted at the factory; she was a body on a production line and nothing more.

"Morning, dear," said Janet, barely looking up from the cake batter she was mixing at the island in the lavish, recently refitted kitchen. "Thought you weren't working today?"

"Apparently, so did Siri. He got confused."

"You don't have a man up there, do you?"

"No, Mum, it's on my phone." Claire put a small cup under the coffee machine she'd brought with her from her old cottage and pressed the double espresso button. "Doesn't matter."

"Because if it were a man, I'd quite like to meet him."

The beans ground and began their slow drip into the cup.

"There is no man, Mum."

If Claire's weight was Janet's first priority, Claire's eternally single status came in a very close second.

"You won't have eggs forever, dear." Janet put the chained reading glasses on the edge of her nose and peered at the recipe she was following. "I'm the only one at the Women's Institute without a grandchild, you know."

"Really?" Claire tossed back the hot espresso – bitter and strong, just what she needed. "Why didn't you mention it?"

Claire pecked her mother on the cheek, grabbed her handbag from the hat stand, and ran out the back door. She'd usually take the front, but it was quicker to cut through the fields behind the cul-de-sac. Ian Baron, the owner of the farm, wouldn't be too pleased if he caught Claire running through his farm again, but the day couldn't get any worse than how it had started.

Except it could.

As her foot sank into the large, warm pile of cow dung, she was forcibly reminded of the other reason she usually chose to walk the long way around.

AFTER A QUICK TEXT MESSAGE, CLAIRE'S UNCLE PAT MET her at the front of the large factory. Much like everything else in Northash, the factory's exterior had remained untouched for over a century.

"I've been covering for you," he said, glancing down at

her foot and already walking back to the factory doors. "What happened?"

"It's been one of those mornings." She jogged to keep up. "Don't ask."

"Said you were at a doctor's appointment. Didn't go into specifics. Nicola didn't ask, not that the Warton Witch seems to care about any of us at this point."

People had been calling Nicola the 'Warton Witch' ever since she took over running the factory after her father's death six months ago. Her ruthless cost-cutting changes hadn't put her at the top of anyone's Christmas card list.

"I won't make a habit of it," Claire said, knowing her uncle was technically her superior in the rank of things. "Messed up my alarm."

"Don't worry, love." Pat chuckled, yanking the front door open for Claire. "Think you might have got away with it this time."

"My foot says overwise."

Uncle Pat, her father's slightly younger brother, looked every inch a Harris. He was just as short and round, with the same thin hair and glasses. He was one of the few people who had worked at the factory longer than Claire, although thanks to his promotion to shift manager five years ago, he was spared having to wear the lumpy blue jumpsuits.

They split up, and he got back to his job, leaving

Claire to quickly clock in. Instead of going straight to her place at the label assembly line, she rushed across the factory floor to the bathrooms and changing rooms on the other side.

Damon Gilbert, the man she worked next to and her only other close friend aside from Sally, gave her a 'where have you been' stare. She waved that she'd explain later.

Claire dug around in the open lockers before moving onto the spare jumpsuits bin, already knowing none would fit her. The sizes were unisex, but most of the women at the factory were smaller than Claire. She wasn't sure she fancied an entire shift with the gusset of a too-small jumpsuit crammed up her behind.

"Where've you been?" Belinda Lang, the woman who usually worked across the assembly line from Claire, appeared from the bathroom, smelling slightly of cigarette smoke – as she did most days. "Nicola was asking around after you."

"Slept in."

"Easily done." Belinda opened her locker and tucked away a packet of cigarettes. "Oh, can you smell that? Smells like…"

"Cow dung." Claire chuckled and nodded down at her foot. "It's me. Cut through the farm."

"Ian wouldn't like that."

"Well, his cows did his dirty work before he had the chance to chase me off with a shotgun." Claire kicked off

17

the shoe, glad she had a spare pair in her locker. "Don't suppose you have a spare jumpsuit, by any chance?"

Belinda, the only other woman bigger than Claire at the factory, pulled a blue jumpsuit from her locker and tossed it across with a smile and a wink.

The spare jumpsuit was far too big and stank of stale smoke, but Claire would take too loose over too tight any day.

BARELY AN HOUR INTO HER WORK, THE BELL RANG TO announce lunch. Most spent their free hour in the windowless canteen and break room. The rest piled into cars and went into the village to eat in the pub or café. Claire and Damon, on the other hand, had their own routine.

Leaving the looming Victorian factory behind, they walked down a short path to the wall bordering Ian's farm, crossing the stream separating the two. As usual, Damon, the taller of the pair (but only by a couple of inches), climbed over first before helping Claire.

The wall wasn't comfortable, but they were high enough to have a view of the whole of Northash. Hot or cold, as long as it was dry, this was where they ate lunch. Claire wouldn't have had it any other way. She'd heard people talk about how strange they were to eat their lunch outside, but personally, she thought it was stranger to spend their one free hour cooped up in a noisy, dim room with bad canteen food.

"Don't tell me your mum's got you on another diet," Damon said, nodding at Claire's empty lap as he dug his usual meal deal out of a supermarket bag. "You can't not eat."

"Forgot to grab something."

Damon pulled out half his sandwich and handed it to her with a smile. She didn't argue, and she knew he didn't mind. Bacon, lettuce, and tomato on white bread. It was a good thing her mother couldn't see them through the fields, though Claire could just make out the back of the cottage from where they sat.

"I went to view the shop again yesterday."

"You're torturing yourself."

"I know."

"Still no closer?"

Claire pulled her phone out and showed Damon her bank balance. £200 down on what she'd shown Sally the day before. If she didn't have the constant reminder, she wouldn't have believed the credit card debt from her early twenties was still following her around.

"You've got more than me." He pulled a tomato slice out of his sandwich and tossed it into the grass before pushing up his glasses with the back of his wrist. "You're lucky you're living at home. Marley's put my rent up again. Can barely afford it as it is. Think I'm going to have to start selling some of my *Doctor Who* collection."

"You wouldn't dare."

"I might not have a choice."

"You'd have more if you made your own lunches."

"Where'd be the fun in that?"

They chuckled and finished eating their halves of the sandwich, staring out at the peaceful countryside with only the mooing of the cows in the fields in front of them to break the silence. Northash might have been an uneventful place to live, but Claire wouldn't have traded it for anything.

Damon joined the factory five years after Claire. He had tried to make it as a journalist in Manchester, but when he lost his first job working for a small newspaper and couldn't find another, he came back with his tail between his legs. After a short, fruitless job hunt, he succumbed to the factory, like people had been doing for the past century. Warton Candle Factory was never anyone's first choice, but it was always there to fall back on.

Being similarly a little too overweight and unlucky in love, they'd quickly gravitated towards each other. Like most people in the village, they'd gone to the same high school, but their paths had rarely crossed until the factory. Damon had spent his school years in the top set with the rest of the brainboxes, whereas Claire had settled for average somewhere in the middle.

While her only other friend, Sally, juggled it all effortlessly, Damon was in the same boat as Claire. Two people in their mid-thirties struggling through adulthood. They knew they were in an ever-shrinking pool of people yet to settle down and find the traditional family life both their mothers would love for them to have.

"I had another sniff of that new vanilla candle the development team have come up with," Damon muttered through his first mouthful of prawn cocktail crisps. He offered the bag to Claire, and she took a couple. "I'm telling you, Claire, Nicola *has* stolen your new scent."

"Not this again."

"It's the *same!*" Damon cried. "She must have got hold of one. Have you sold any?"

Claire shook her head. She'd given a couple away. One to Sally, one to Damon, and some to family – all people she'd never ask to pay, no matter how badly she needed the extra income.

"Well, it's identical." Damon finished the crisps and folded the packet carefully before knotting it like he always did. "She's stolen your scent formula."

Some people kept a little black book full of contacts. Claire's had all her scent formulas in it. And she'd lost it. She had no idea where she could have misplaced it, but she hadn't seen it in weeks. Too embarrassed to admit Nicola might have found out that way, Claire hadn't brought herself to tell Damon about the missing notebook.

"Maybe."

"There's no *maybe* about it." He sighed. "It's the *exact* same. Your vanilla candle is the nicest I've ever smelt. It's unique. Too unique to suddenly show up here two weeks later."

"Could be a coincidence."

"Pfft." Damon nudged her with his shoulder. "She's your mother's neighbour, isn't she? Surely you could talk to her."

"They're not those kinds of neighbours."

"Well, if I were you, I'd confront her."

Claire groaned. She had never been the confrontational type. She always kept herself to herself and got on with her work.

But she knew Damon was right.

The candle was identical.

Claire knew she couldn't own a formula for a vanilla candle, but the scent was scarily accurate. She had spent six months testing different fragrance oils in different quantities, determined to create a perfect vanilla candle different from everything else on the market. It hadn't been an easy task, and she'd been so proud when she reached the version she deemed to be perfect.

"I suppose I could."

"Go on then." Damon checked his watch after dusting the crumbs out of his short beard. "You've still got forty-five minutes before we're back to work."

"What? Now?"

"You know it's better to catch her at lunch than at the end of the day." Damon jumped off the wall. "She zooms off in that flashy sportscar before anyone can catch her. I'll come with you for moral support."

"Damon, I—"

"You deserve the credit." He nodded for her to jump down. "C'mon, Claire. Do you want to open your own candle shop one day or not? If Nicola has somehow stolen your candle, which she *has*, you at least deserve to be paid what the development team are being paid. They're on three quid an hour more than us! Do you know how much extra that is a week?"

"No."

"Well, neither do I, but I'm guessing it's a lot."

Claire huffed as she swung her legs back over the wall. Damon held his hand out and helped her jump down. They walked back to the factory, but Claire had no intention of confronting Nicola.

Not like this, at least.

She and Nicola barely said two words to each other at work, and even less back at the cul-de-sac. Nicola and her husband, Graham, had lived next door to her parents for years, but the couple kept themselves to themselves, despite Janet's best efforts to incorporate them into cul-de-sac events.

"Damon, I don't think I—"

"What the heck!"

Damon held his arm out in front of Claire as they walked across the courtyard in front of the factory. He nodded up to the window of Nicola's office, but Claire's eyes had already taken in what Damon was seeing.

Nicola was kissing a man right by the high window, and without needing to get any closer, Claire knew the man wasn't her husband.

Graham was a quiet man, no taller than five foot five, and as thin as a pencil. Geeky-looking, Claire's mother had always said, and perfect for his job as an accountant. The man Nicola was kissing was tall, broad, and had a headful of thick hair.

Nicola pulled away from the man and spun, her bright red curls spinning with her. She took a step away from the man, her hand resting on her head. The man reached out, but Nicola pulled away before his fingers touched her arm. She turned to the window, her eyes landing on Claire and Damon immediately.

"Crap," Damon whispered, dropping his head.

"Crap, indeed."

They hurried into the shadow of the factory, out of sight of the window.

"That was Jeff," Damon said. "The health and safety manager."

"I know." Claire looked down at her uniform. "I'm wearing his wife's spare jumpsuit."

"Claire, you know what this means, don't you?" Damon whispered, pulling her further into the shadow of the looming chimney.

"That Belinda's husband is cheating on her.

"Well, yes."

"She idolises him."

"I know." Damon shook his head. "But forget about Belinda for a second. Think about Nicola. You have something on her now."

"Damon..."

"*What!*"

"I'm not going to blackmail our boss!"

"Then blackmail your neighbour." Damon huffed and grabbed her by the arms. "You know as well as I do how much money Nicola stands to make off a newly improved vanilla scent. We sell to companies all over the country, and they're all going to want it. *Your* scent, Claire. She's going to make thousands upon thousands, you're going to be stuck on this assembly line next to me, and someone else is going to get that shop. How long has it been since the last shop came up?"

Claire swallowed and thought back. She'd been down

this road before, viewing what was now a bookshop, dreaming of her candle shop.

"Two years."

"You willing to wait for another two?"

Claire shook her head.

"Then talk to her." Damon yanked open the door and nodded for her to go in. "Besides, she saw us looking. It's hardly blackmailing if she knows we know. She might hand over a bag of cash just to shut you up."

They walked through the quiet reception area and onto the large factory floor. The place was deserted. The jumbled-up chatter of conversations floated from behind the doors of the canteen.

They craned their necks to look up at Nicola's office, which sat at the front of the building and had a large window to look out at the factory floor as everyone worked. A metal walkway ran along the edge of the open second floor, with a couple of offices dotted along each side before meeting at the opposite end in the central metal staircase.

"Damon, I can't do this," Claire whispered, jogging to keep up with him as he marched to the stairs. "It's not—"

Before Claire could finish her sentence, the sound of smashing glass filled the empty, cavernous factory. Claire spun towards the sound. As though in slow motion, she watched Nicola fly from the office in a flurry of shattered glass and red hair, hands grasping for something that wasn't there.

Nicola landed with a deafening thud on the production line, her back bent in an entirely unnatural way. She didn't even cry out in pain; she lay like an abandoned rag doll, limbs limp, with sparkling shards of glass all around her.

Claire and Damon stared at each other blankly as the canteen doors burst open. Dozens of sets of eyes looked up at the frame where the window used to be, but whoever had pushed their boss to her death was already long gone.

CHAPTER THREE

Sat in the corner of her father's shed at the bottom of the garden, the plant pot provided a firm seat for Claire. Hunched over, she didn't fit as easily as she had as a child, but she still loved watching her father's green thumbs working their magic as much as she had when she had to clamber atop the plant pot.

Stress usually led Claire to her candle workshop in the bedroom, or perhaps to her favourite candle shop in Skipton, but the current writhing in her stomach went far beyond stress.

She hadn't been able to stop seeing Nicola Warton spread over the assembly line like an uncooked slab of meat every time she blinked her eyes.

"Done." Her father presented the re-potted infant rosebush, his fingers caked in mud. "What do you think?"

"Lovely."

"It's for one of your mother's Women's Institute friends." He cocked his head, examining his handiwork. "She said my roses were the best she'd ever seen, so we came to a little deal. One clipping to grow in her garden in exchange for four pots of that delicious raspberry jam she makes."

Claire loved Mrs Knowles' raspberry jam as much as her father did. They always stocked up when she sold it at the church fêtes. Despite her mother's warning about sugar, nothing tasted nicer on hot buttered toast than Mrs Knowles' raspberry jam.

But Claire couldn't face the thought of eating. Few times in her life had her mood affected her appetite; this was one of them.

The clouds cleared, and the afternoon sun streamed through the tiny, streaky window. It landed on her father's almost bald head, illuminating the large square scar on his scalp that had forced him into retirement.

Alan had gone to see the doctor because of his constant headaches. Three weeks later, he'd been on the operating table having a brain tumour removed. Benign, they'd called it, but not small enough to leave alone. Not small enough to stop their lives grinding to a screeching halt.

Claire hadn't been able to eat much through that whole ordeal either.

Knuckles rapped firmly against the wood, and the door opened immediately. Claire's mother stood in the doorway, arms folded, her apron covered in flour.

"One of your old work friends is here," she said to Alan, nodding back at the cottage. "Detective something or other. Fat fella. Looks like he's wearing a toupee."

"That'll be Harry Ramsbottom." A smile pricked up the corners of his lips. They dropped almost immediately, and he turned to Claire with a sympathetic smile. "That'll be for you, dear. Remember what I told you, and you'll be fine. DI Ramsbottom is one of the nice ones."

Claire forced herself up off the plant pot. She'd hoped she could spend the day hiding in her father's shed. She glanced at her watch. 4:30 pm. If the factory hadn't closed, she'd still be at work, applying labels to the latest batch of Sea Breeze candles for one of their large, south-coast clients.

DI Ramsbottom perched on the edge of her father's favourite armchair by the fireplace, dunking a plain digestive into a cup of tea. The toupee was obvious, the top far too golden brown for the grey sides. Did he not know everyone could tell, or did he simply not care? Claire vaguely remembered him from some of the police functions she'd attended with her father, but she couldn't recall ever speaking to him.

"Ah, Claire!" Harry wiped the crumbs from his chest,

where his shirt buttons strained to contain his stomach. "How are you holding up, my dear?"

"As well as can be."

"Terrible incident." He motioned for Claire to sit on the armchair across from him. "Quite shocking, actually. Life can be so cruel. Killed your boss and your neighbour with one big stone."

"We weren't close," Claire's mother said, hurrying into the sitting room to push more digestives from the packet onto the plate. "Frosty woman. Never said much to us. Could barely raise a smile."

Janet sat on the edge of the sofa next to Claire. She pulled Claire's hand from her mouth; she hadn't even realised she'd been biting her nails.

"Good to see you again, Harry." Alan stood in the doorway, looking out of breath as he leaned against the frame. "How's the old station?"

"Oh, you know." Harry nodded his head from side to side; the toupee didn't move. "Same old, same old – although, this murder has got everyone running around like headless chickens! Quite a change of pace." He paused to shovel down another biscuit. "How's the…" Harry's finger wafted up to the toupee. "The … Oh, what's the politically correct thing to say?"

"Brain tumour." Alan always smiled the same tight smile whenever the topic came up. "Coping as well as I can. Left leg hasn't been the same since. Had to get an automatic car. Can't quite handle the clutch. The doctor said the removal must have caused a little nerve damage, but I'm sure I'll be as right as rain in no time."

"Terrible business." Harry dunked another biscuit into his tea the way a chain smoker burned through cigarettes. "We all said it couldn't have happened to a nicer bloke. Life can be so cruel, can't it?"

"It can." Alan's smiled tightened even further. "Janet, dear?"

"Hmmm?"

"Why don't you come and help me in the kitchen?"

Claire's mother adjusted the hem of her apron. She sighed, slapped her knees, and stood, dumping out the last of the biscuits before she left. Nobody loved eavesdropping more than Janet.

"So," DI Ramsbottom began, pulling a small notepad from his strained top pocket. "You saw it happen, is that correct?"

Claire nodded, wishing she had a cup of tea to reach for, if only for something to do with her hands. The ends of her nails found their way back into her mouth.

"And you told the officer on the scene that you didn't see who could have pushed the woman?"

"That's correct." Claire forced her hands out of her mouth and into her lap. "Damon and I were—"

"Damon Gilbert?" He flipped back in his pad. "Your colleague?"

"And friend."

"Colleague *and* friend." He jotted down the detail as though it mattered. "You were coming from your lunch break, and you saw someone push Nicola."

"Not exactly." Claire inhaled, the image still vivid in her mind. "We were walking into the factory. We eat our lunch outside when the weather is nice. Everyone else was in the canteen, so it was just us in the factory. We didn't actually see that she was pushed because we had our backs to the window. We turned around when we heard the glass smash, and we saw her fall and … and land. When we looked up, nobody was there."

"And you didn't see anyone run out?"

Claire shook her head.

"And you didn't see anyone in the office with her?"

Claire went to shake her head again, but she remembered what her father had said about telling the truth. She'd left out the kissing detail when she'd talked to the officer at the scene, more out of shock than anything. Her father had spent too many years in the force to give her bad advice.

"When we were outside, Damon and I, we saw Nicola with someone in the office," Claire started, her nails back in her mouth. "A man. They were kissing."

"And I assume from your tone that this *man* wasn't her husband?"

"No, he wasn't."

Janet gasped in the kitchen.

"Do you know who the man was?"

"Jeff," Claire said, watching as he scribbled the name down. "Jeff Lang. He works at the factory. Health and safety manager. Comes in once a week for inspections."

"How well do you know Jeff?"

"Not at all, but I work across from his wife on the line." Claire inhaled, twisting her hands in her lap. "Belinda Lang. She's a nice woman. She just turned fifty the other week. The way she always talked about Jeff, I thought they were happy."

"Hmmm." Harry scribbled down the details before reaching out for another biscuit. "So, you saw Nicola kissing this Jeff fella, and then you went straight into the factory?"

"No." Claire shook her head. "We talked outside for a couple of minutes."

"We?"

"Damon and me."

"What were you talking about?"

Claire thought about telling the truth, but she didn't think Damon's half-baked, slapped-together blackmail plan was relevant anymore.

"Work stuff."

"I see."

"We were still on our break," she explained. "We get an hour."

"More than most places."

Most people said that. William Warton had always been very insistent about giving his staff an uninterrupted paid hour for lunch, even if the law said he only had to give thirty minutes. Everyone had expected Nicola to slash the breaks like she had the work hours, but she either hadn't wanted to or hadn't got around to it before her death.

"Well, you've given us some lines of inquiry to look into." He slapped the pad shut and picked up the rest of the biscuits, which he wrapped in a handkerchief and secreted in his pocket. "If you think of anything else, I'm sure your father can tell you who to call."

DI Ramsbottom forced himself out of the chair, the effort reddening his round face. He nodded at her, and she almost expected him to tip his toupee.

After a brief round of goodbyes and promises to catch up with Alan over a pint sometime soon, Detective Inspector Harry Ramsbottom showed himself out and struggled into a tiny two-seater Smart car. As he drove away, Claire couldn't help but think he looked like a clown in a tiny circus car.

"Well, well, well." Claire's mother grinned ear to ear, foot tapping, arms folded. "Nicola and Belinda's husband. I wonder what Graham would have to say about that."

"The man has just lost his wife." Alan rested a hand on

her shoulder. "Let's give him a few days to adjust before we start the gossiping, eh, dear?"

"I'm not a gossip."

"And the Pope isn't Catholic," Claire said, almost to herself. "I – I'm going out for a walk."

"A *walk?*" Janet cried, yanking her watch around her wrist. "There's a cottage pie in the oven!"

Claire grabbed her light denim jacket and stuffed her feet into her comfiest trainers.

"You're always telling me I should get more exercise."

"This is no time to get smart, dear!"

"I'll be back in time for the cottage pie."

Claire didn't linger, leaving before her mother could tie her to a dining room chair. Not that she wasn't thrilled by the idea of her mother's cottage pie – one of the few things Janet could make without burning – but she couldn't face the inevitable barrage of her mother's questions.

Claire wasn't sure why she went to the empty shop, but that's where she found herself, staring through the window, her bespectacled reflection staring back. Her thin mousy hair, cut just below her jaw, needed a trim, but she'd been putting it off so she could save as much money as possible.

She laughed.

It would take more than a few haircuts to save up the money she needed to put down a deposit and first month's rent for the shop. And that didn't even include how much it would cost to turn the place from an empty café into a fully stocked candle shop. Not to mention the lights, and water, and business rates, and tax.

"A pipe dream," she muttered, locking eyes with her reflection. "Time to give it up, Claire."

She turned away from the shop, not even knowing if she'd have a job to go back to. She was due in tomorrow at 9 am, but nobody had any idea if the factory would even open. The work's group chat hadn't stopped pinging all afternoon, but Claire didn't have the energy to look at the stream of speculation and worry.

Out of the corner of her eye, she spotted Damon exiting the fish and chip shop next door, a heavy-looking plastic bag in hand. He lived in the flat above the vegan café, in the opposite direction, but he looked up the street, catching her eye. He didn't seem to think twice before walking over.

"I couldn't face the thought of cooking." He held up the bag. "I think I ordered one of everything. Don't suppose you want to split it? Might make me feel better."

"Mum's got a cottage pie in the oven."

"And just like that, life goes on," he said, a sad smile lingering. "How are you feeling?"

"Strange."

"Have the police been to see you?"

"Just now."

Damon let out a relieved looking sigh. "I thought it was just me. They were asking all these questions like I was trying to hide something."

"Were you honest?"

"Probably too honest." He looked around the quiet square. "I told them about what we *saw*. The kissing. Should I have kept my mouth shut?"

"Don't worry, I told them too. My dad said I should be honest, so I was."

"You didn't tell them that I—"

"Wanted to blackmail our now-deceased boss on my behalf?" Claire chuckled. "No, I didn't see the point. We didn't get that far, did we? And besides, we were together when she was pushed. We're each other's alibis."

"Oh yeah." Damon scratched the side of his head with his free hand. "I didn't think of it like that."

"But we're the only eyewitnesses," Claire explained. "Dad said they'll probably keep asking us questions, hoping we'll remember some forgotten detail so they can unravel the mystery."

"And do you think *he* did it?" Damon gulped, looking around again. "Jeff?"

"I don't know, but I'd guess he's at the station right now. Since we both saw him kissing Nicola right before she died, he'll be suspect number one."

"You sound like you know what you're talking about."

"That's what happens when you grow up with a dad in the police."

"My dad's a butcher, and I couldn't tell you the difference between braising steak and fillet." Damon glanced down at this bag. "I've always been more of a fish and chips man anyway. Sure you don't want to ditch the parents for an early fish supper?"

Claire glanced at the lane that would take her back to the cul-de-sac. As tempting an offer as it was, she shook her head.

"I can't risk being made homeless as well as unemployed." She sucked the air through her teeth. "We might not have a job to go back to, and any chance of that pay rise went out of the window with—"

"With Nicola," Damon finished her sentence for her. "No pun intended, right?"

"Perhaps I should choose my words more carefully."

"Why?" Damon rolled his eyes. "The woman still *stole* your candle formula!"

"We don't—"

"Yes, we do." Damon pulled his phone from his pocket. "I know you were worried about not having proof, but I saw this on my phone earlier."

Damon tapped a couple of things before turning the phone to Claire. She looked at the picture of the final vanilla candle, remembering the image instantly. She'd sent it the moment she'd finished the winning batch a little under a month ago, knowing she'd finally achieved what she set out to do.

"Unless your phone has smell-o-vision, I don't know how that helps me."

"Look closer." Damon pinched the screen, zooming into the dressing table behind the candle. "Your little black book of formulas is there, open to the vanilla page. Can't quite make out the measurements, but you can see the title."

"Since when did cameras on phones get so clear?" Claire squinted at the image. "That's it."

"Good, isn't it?" Damon grinned. "You know me. I'm a tech geek. Only the best for me. The image data has the time and date on it too, which puts it two weeks before the new samples made the rounds at the factory."

"So?"

"Claire." Damon huffed. "It's proof *you* came up with it. That's your handwriting on an image pre-dating the samples. I'd bet my chippy supper the factory can't pull up any proof dated earlier than this."

"I lost the book a few days after I took that picture," Claire confessed. "I have no idea how, but it vanished into thin air. The samples came out of the development lab less than a week later."

"Exactly!" Damon tucked his phone away. "You can sue."

"Sue, who? She's dead!"

"Did the factory close when William died? No, it passed to his daughter, Nicola. Someone else will step in. Nicola's husband would be the next of kin, right? And she has that brother?"

"Ben Warton?" Claire remembered aloud. "Isn't he in prison?"

"Got out last month, apparently." Damon glanced down at his bag of food, and Claire was sure she heard his stomach growl. "Listen, don't give up just yet, okay? Whoever takes over, they might be more understanding than Nicola. You deserve what's yours, Claire."

They parted ways with a promise to keep each other in the loop. She waited until Damon disappeared into his flat on the other side of the square before turning back to the empty shop.

A flicker of hope surged through her chest against her will. She sighed, knowing she couldn't let go of the dream.

"But I'm still no closer," she whispered to her reflection before setting off home.

CHAPTER FOUR

The days following Nicola's death dragged by slowly. No one was charged with her murder, and the factory doors remained shut.

The group chat continued to whip itself into a frenzy with every passing hour without news. Some were talking about finding other jobs, others trying to organise a revolt to throw open the doors and continue working despite their lack of a leader. Not until Claire added her Uncle Pat to the group on Thursday night was there any sense of order.

"Let's all meet for a drink," he'd written. "Seven at The Hesketh Arms on Friday night. We'll get to the bottom of this, one way or another."

Things calmed down a little after that, and along with the other hundred or so factory employees, Claire found herself crammed in The Hesketh Arms on Friday night. Theresa and Malcolm Richards, the landlords of the pub, ran out of their locally famous Hesketh Homebrew before the clock reached seven.

Claire and Damon arrived together at half-past six, just in time to slide into the last two free seats in the corner of the tiny pub. Gentrification had swept through most pubs up and down the country, but not in Northash. The Hesketh Arms had kept it's dated carpet, picture-cluttered exposed stone walls, and mismatching furniture. The scent of beer clung to everything, and passing tourists would probably dismiss it as a 'dump,' but the locals knew better. The homebrew was the best for miles around, the food was fresh and homemade, and Theresa and Malcolm's hospitality couldn't be beaten.

"Do you think they're serving food?" Damon asked, casting his eye over the expansive menu. "I could eat a small horse."

"Don't you dare." Claire pulled the menu from him. "They're rushed off their feet."

Even with an overwhelmingly full pub and only the two of them to serve every thirsty customer, their smiles never faltered. Claire had heard locals refer to Theresa and Malcolm as the mother and father of Northash, and tonight, more than ever, she understood why.

When the clock struck seven, the door finally stopped opening and closing. Claire recognised every face; she'd worked with most of these people for years. If the factory didn't re-open, she wouldn't be the only one without a job. As much as people had moaned and griped about how Nicola had run the factory since old William's death, they all needed their jobs. Without the factory, Northash's sturdy economy would collapse in a heartbeat. The couple of jobs that came up here and there weren't enough to satisfy the demand.

At ten past seven, Uncle Pat emerged from the crowd, using a chair to boost himself above the heads. A quick round of shushing rippled around the pub until all eyes were fixed on Pat.

"Looks like we're all here," he started, smiling and nodding around the room. "Thanks to Theresa and Malcolm for letting us have our meeting here. If you haven't already, throw a couple of quid into the tip jar if you can spare it. I'm sure they'd appreciate it."

Pat tipped his pint to the bar, and Theresa and Malcolm smiled around their full pub. Those close to the tip jar tossed in a couple of coins, and everyone else, including Claire, pulled out a couple to add in on their way out.

"We all know why we're here," Pat continued, his eyes catching Claire's as he scanned the room. "I'm afraid I've been kept as much in the dark as the rest of you. I've tried to talk to Nicola's husband, Graham, but understandably, he's shut down since his wife's … death."

"Murder," someone shouted out. "Call it what it was."

"Yes, you're right." Pat nodded before sipping the foamy head of his beer. "Nicola was murdered, and the police don't seem to be doing much to catch whoever pushed her through that window. But that's not why we're here, is it? We're not here to gossip about who killed Nicola, and regardless of when or if that person is caught, we're still none the wiser about the status of our jobs. We're all in the same boat."

"No, we're not," another called out. "I'm on minimum wage. I'm living hand to mouth."

"I can't afford to feed my cats."

"I can't afford to feed my *kids*!"

The shouting continued until Claire couldn't make out individual words anymore. She sipped her beer, eyes fixed on her uncle, wishing everyone else would do the same. Pat had always been well-respected in the factory. His promotion to shift manager hadn't been by accident. He was a natural leader, and everyone knew it.

"Yes, yes!" he boomed, hushing the crowd with his hands. "Whether it's your plants, your pets, or your children, we've all got responsibilities! And, yes, some of us might be on slightly higher wages, but that doesn't mean we're not in the same boat. I might be one of your shift managers, but I'm sixty years old, barely have any savings, and that government pension is still years away. I want to get to the bottom of this as much as you do, which is why I called this meeting. We're all being left in the dark, and none of us knows what's going on."

"So, what do we do?" someone called out. "C'mon, Pat! Tell us what to do."

"I – I don't know." Pat's face turned bright red. "But if we put our heads together, we can come up with something, I'm sure."

"I don't believe this," a woman shouted, standing up, handbag over her shoulder. "I had to pay a babysitter to watch my kids, and for what? To *speculate* about our future? I thought you'd have *answers* for us!"

"He's only a shift manager," Claire found herself calling out. "Like he said, we're all in the same boat."

The woman, who Claire assumed was quite new since she didn't recognise her, sat back down, handbag still tight to her shoulder.

"The police released the factory days ago," Pat continued after gulping down more of his pint. "We could go back to work at any time, but nobody is in charge."

"Then *take* charge!"

"Yeah, let's just do it ourselves."

"We need lawyers."

"Yeah, we must have rights!"

The front door opened, and a sharp-suited, redheaded man walked in, silencing the pub.

"Bloody hell!" Damon whispered, choking on his beer. "I think that's Ben Warton!"

Even though the man standing in the doorway looked much older than the image in her memory, Claire instantly recognised him. Ben had been a couple of years ahead of her at school. He'd been a heartthrob to most girls, and even Claire had fancied him at one point – from a distance. He had the classic Warton good looks, with short, thick, red curls, and a jawline that could slice a candle right down the middle. Even tipping forty and clearly not as fresh as he'd once been, he was still undeniably handsome, especially in his tailored suit.

"Having a cosy little meeting?" he called out, revealing that a front tooth had been replaced with one of dazzling gold. "Nice of you to invite me."

"Who are you?" someone shouted above the whispering.

"That's *Ben Warton!*" someone else replied. "Fresh from prison, by the looks of it."

"*Falsely* accused," Ben insisted as the crowd parted around him. He made his way to Pat, still standing on the chair in front of the fireplace. "I'll take it from here, Pat."

"Ex-excuse me?"

"The meeting." Ben nodded for Pat to get down, and like a lap dog, her uncle obeyed. "That's why you're all here, isn't it? To figure out the fate of the factory?"

Ben climbed up onto the chair, his head almost

touching the low beams; Pat had been nowhere near. He looked out around the crowd as people chattered. He planted his hands on his hips and sighed, reminding Claire of a teacher waiting for the class to be quiet. Somehow, his effortless swagger silenced the room.

"My sister is dead," he stated, voice devoid of warmth. "Murdered, they're saying. I'm not going to lie and say we were close. We weren't. In fact, I'd go as far as to say I hated her, and I'm sure I'm not the only one here. I might have spent the past decade locked up, but I know what she was like. I know she was running that factory into the ground." He looked around the room, smiling at his audience. "I can see it in your eyes. My father never wanted *her* to have it. Even with me behind bars, he wanted to leave it to *me*, but he couldn't. Not legally, anyway. Nicola never wanted to run the factory; she just didn't want me to have it."

"Why was he locked up?" Damon whispered to Claire when Ben paused for breath.

"Can't remember," Claire admitted. "Must have been serious to get ten years."

Ben let the whispering build up for a moment before planting his hands and sighing again, once more effectively silencing the pub. Like his father, an undeniable air of authority clung to his red curls and the set of his jaw.

"Warton Candle Factory has been feeding the families

of Northash since 1890," Ben announced, dropping his arms by his side. "My great-great-great-grandfather, Charles Warton, loved this village more than anyone. He gave us industry, and generations of my family have kept that going, as it should be. When I got out, I talked to my sister and tried to make her see sense, but her mind was made up. Typical Nicola."

"About what?" someone called out.

"Selling the factory." Ben's eyes darkened. "She was going to sell the place so she could run away with the money."

Shocked gasps and startled conversation rippled around the pub, the noise growing to a deafening level. Claire kept her eyes on Ben's face. Even though he was trying his best to maintain his tough expression, the flicker of a smile at the corners of his mouth was unmistakable.

"Fear not!" he cried, clapping his hands together and silencing everyone in an instant. "She never got that far. Karma made sure of that."

"But the factory is still closed!"

"Not anymore." Ben grinned around the pub. "I will continue the mission set out by Charles Warton. The factory doors will re-open tomorrow with a *true* Warton running things, as it should always have been. We're going to turn things around together! Who's with me?"

The talk started up immediately, and it only took one

person to start clapping before a rapturous round of applause filled the tiny pub. Ben grinned, arms folded tight against his chest, as he lapped it up. Even Damon clapped, but Claire's hands remained wrapped around her pint glass.

"I suggest you all drink up and get an early night," Ben called out when the noise died down. "We've got a lot to catch up on."

And just like that, the tense atmosphere vanished. Ben climbed down from the chair, and the crowd parted around him like he was a rock star. Hands slapped his back, and people fought over who was going to buy him his first drink at the bar.

"That was bloody weird," Damon said after draining his pint. "Shall we make a move? I don't fancy sticking around for the after-party."

Claire nodded and drained the rest of her drink. Half the crowd seemed eager to leave, while the others appeared keen to celebrate with their new leader. Claire wasn't sure if it was her imagination, but there seemed to be a definite male and female divide between the two groups.

They followed the flow out of the pub and into the night. Outside, she found her Uncle Pat amongst the crowd of people saying their goodbyes and going their separate ways.

"Well, it's a result, I suppose," Pat said to Claire when

he made his way over. "Not what I was expecting, but it's something."

"Weird, though, don't you think?" Claire whispered to him, spotting the same concern she felt on the faces around her. "All that stuff about hating Nicola and her wanting to sell the factory?"

"A little," he nodded his head side to side. "If your father were here, I'm sure he'd say it sounded like a motive."

Before Claire could agree with him, she spotted Belinda by the pub door, a cigarette clamped in her mouth while shaky hands attempted to light it.

"Terrible habit," Pat whispered, nodding at Belinda. "Especially at her age. Glad I quit when I did. I bet she's the one always secretly smoking in the women's bathrooms. Nicola was on the warpath about that."

Claire barely remembered the days when her father and uncle used to smoke cigarettes. They'd quit together when Claire was a little girl, so she hadn't grown up around it. Like most, Claire had tried it while still in school. It had been Sally's idea, and it hadn't taken long for someone to point them toward the older girls hanging out in a smoke cloud behind the science block at lunch. They each handed over 50p and received a single cigarette, which they had attempted to share. One badly inhaled puff had been enough to put them off for life.

Claire's addiction of choice was candles, and she

couldn't imagine having to give them up. At least they were only bad for her bank account and not her health. Not until she'd started working at the factory had she realised so many people still partook of the habit.

"Are you okay, Belinda?" Claire asked when she was close enough to speak without raising her voice. "Your hands are shaking."

Belinda sucked hard on her cigarette, her eyes staring deep into Claire's. The fine lines etched around her lips made her look much older than her fifty years, and the nicotine-yellowed teeth didn't help matters. Belinda's usual jolly smile was nowhere to be seen today. No matter how she answered the question, Claire knew she wasn't fine.

"It's all been a lot to take in." Belinda let the smoke trickle through her nostrils. "Nicola dying, now this. All week, I've been worried sick about losing my job. Emotional whiplash."

"That's one way to put it." Claire offered a supportive smile. "If there is something, you can talk to me. You know that, right? How many years have we worked together?"

"Too many." Belinda's lips formed a thin smile around the cigarette, but her eyes still brimmed with worry. "I'm fine, honestly. You in tomorrow?"

"Nine to five."

"I'll see you tomorrow, then."

Belinda skulked off, cigarette still held between her pursed lips. She pushed through the lingering crowd, not seeming to care about the people she banged into on the way.

"What was that about?" Damon asked when Claire joined him by the kerb.

"I wanted to see if she was all right, considering."

"Oh, yeah." Damon clicked his fingers. "Jeff. Does she know about the affair?"

"She didn't say, and I didn't ask." Claire looked down the street and watched as Belinda turned the corner, leaving a cloud of smoke in the warm glow of the streetlamp. "Her nerves seem shot to smithereens."

"Police probably told her." Damon checked his watch. "Fancy a film at mine? I think I need another drink after all that. I have some cans of that toffee apple cider you like in the fridge."

"Another night." Claire patted him on the arm. "There's someone I need to talk to."

SAT ON THE UPTURNED PLANT POT IN THE CORNER OF HER father's dark shed, Claire finally paused for breath after recounting as much of the meeting as she could remember. She waited for him to say something, but as usual, he considered his words carefully before jumping in.

"I think you're right to be suspicious," he said finally. "It looks like you've already identified two people, each with a potential motive."

"So, what do we do?"

He smiled softly, his wrinkles looking deeper than usual in the glow of the moon.

"We do nothing," he said. "It sounds like, for now, you have your job back. It's best to keep your head down and get on."

"Is that what you'd do if you were still a detective?" Claire edged forward. "Ignore the obvious and keep your head down?"

"I'm retired, Claire." He pointed up to his scar, his smile widening. "Mr Tumour saw to that."

"I know you hate retirement."

"Is it that obvious?"

"To me, yes."

"You could always read me like a book, Claire."

"Is DI Ramsbottom up to this case?"

"No." He shook his head. "Nice fella, but he's more interested in the easy life. I suspect he'll coast this case until the book gets passed or something falls into his lap."

Claire's thoughts swirled, and she almost didn't want to speak the words on the tip of her tongue, but she couldn't hold them in.

"I'm going to look into it," Claire said firmly, sitting up straight.

"Claire, you—"

"I saw it happen, Dad," she interrupted. "I'm not the only person who can't afford to lose this job if it all goes wrong."

"You know we'd never see you without."

"I know." Claire smiled. "But not everyone else is so lucky. There are people with kids. I work with these people. I *know* these people. Heck, you know most of them too."

He paused and considered his words again.

"What are you suggesting, exactly?"

"We investigate," she whispered, clutching his hands in hers. "Unofficially and quietly."

"Claire, I can't—"

"Your foot," she said. "I know. I'm not asking you to go chasing suspects across rooftops, I only want to borrow your brain. You're a detective whether you like it or not, Dad. One last case for old time's sake, eh?"

He exhaled heavily, his fingers tightening around hers. He lowered his head, and the divot of his scar was particularly jarring, highlighted by the moon's icy light.

"Something tells me you're going to try to do this with or without my help." He smiled. "You get your stubbornness from your mother."

Claire frowned at the comparison before asking, "Is that a yes?"

"Nothing dangerous." His eyes locked on hers. "Nothing illegal."

"Of course."

They shared the same excited smile.

"And whatever you do," he said, slowly standing, "please don't tell your mother."

CHAPTER FIVE

ver her seventeen years at the factory, Claire's training had covered almost every aspect of candle production. She was in the handful of people who could be moved around the factory, easily adapting to each process and machine. Of course, she liked some jobs more than others. She found gluing wicks into jars and quality control the most boring, but she'd do them if needed.

For the past few years, she had mainly worked on the label sticking station. Others often looked down on this as the easiest job, but those who worked there knew the importance of their role in the overall process. If the labels weren't straight, they wouldn't pass quality control, and they'd be off to the rejects bin. Either the label would have to be painstakingly removed and reapplied, or the candle sold at a discounted rate to the client of that production run.

Claire was quite proud of how few rejects she produced. After years of practise, she had an accurate eye and a steady hand. Her labels were usually straight and free of air bubbles. Today, however, she'd sent down more rejects than she cared to acknowledge, and she wasn't the only one.

"We can't keep up with this speed!" Damon cried over the noise of the wax-pouring machine one station down, slapping another wonky label to a candle. "They're firing them down too quick!"

Claire glanced further up the production line to the wick-sticking station. They were gluing wicks into the mason jars and shooting them down faster than they ever had. Very few had wicks glued accurately in the middle of the jar, as they should be. Nobody was purposefully trying to be bad at their job, but accuracy was hard when they were expected to get through a week's worth of work in one day. It didn't help that Nicola's brother, Ben, and her widowed husband, Graham, had been arguing loudly in the office all morning.

Claire couldn't stop her eyes drifting up to the newly fitted glass window every time the volume rose, and she wasn't the only one.

If the quality of their work mattered, nobody was around to tell them otherwise. The quality control team had been drafted to pack boxes, and the shift managers ran around problem-solving instead of managing. At noon, when the automatic bell rang for lunch, nobody even pretended they were going to linger around to work through their break. Every machine stopped, and the factory floor cleared in record time.

After retrieving their lunches from their lockers, Claire and Damon left the factory for the peaceful solitude of their wall.

"I feel like I'm breathing for the first time today," Damon said, inhaling the crisp afternoon air. "We can't keep going like that. They're going to have to drop some orders, or at least delay them."

"I think Ben is too wrapped up in arguing with Graham to notice how bad things are."

"I'm starving." Damon fished a cheese and ham sandwich, a packet of cheese and onion crisps, and a small bottle of orange juice from his supermarket bag. "Could you hear what they were arguing about?"

Claire pulled out the plastic box her mother had handed her that morning. She usually made her own lunches, but she'd been so distracted while getting ready she'd almost left the house without a thing to eat. She looked at the chicken salad, wishing she had a sandwich and a packet of crisps.

"At least she put some cheese and croutons in." Claire dug around in the salad, hoping to find a secret chocolate bar smuggled at the bottom. "And no, I couldn't hear a word over the machines."

"What do you think they were arguing about?"

"Power?" Claire shrugged. "My dad said Graham has the best legal claim to the factory since he was Nicola's next of kin."

"But Ben is a Warton."

"It's just a name."

"Yeah, the name cast in iron above the factory gates." Damon finished his first sandwich half and immediately picked up the second. "It's his family's factory. Has been since the dawn of time. Surely that must mean something?"

"Usually, I suppose." Claire reached into her handbag and pulled out the folded piece of paper she had printed off late last night in her parents' dedicated computer room. "The reason Ben Warton spent so long in prison. I vaguely remembered bits of the story. It makes for quite an interesting read."

Damon scanned over the *Northash Observer* newspaper article from 2010. In the picture accompanying the article, Ben Warton was the fresher, younger version Claire remembered more vividly.

"Wow," he muttered through his sandwich. "Fraud, theft, and attempted murder? Why is no one talking about this?"

"People have short memories." Claire took the article

back and scanned it. "But it seems Ben's claims that his father wanted him to run the factory aren't quite true. Did you see this quote from William Warton? 'I've no doubt my son was trying to kill me for his own financial gain.'"

"Imagine your own son trying to kill you." Damon unscrewed his orange juice. "Why would Ben do that?"

"That article didn't go into it, but I kept digging. William seemed to think Ben wanted him out of the way so he could inherit the factory and the family money by default, as he's the eldest child. Switched out his blood pressure pills and drove William to the edge of a heart attack."

"What a psycho!"

"He pled not guilty." Claire pointed to Ben's statement in the article. "Seemed to think his sister stitched him up and that she was the one trying to kill their father, but nobody believed him. Nicola even testified against him in the trial."

"Must have been convincing enough for the jury if he got ten years."

"Twenty," Claire corrected. "Got out in half the time because he convinced a parole board he was a changed man. Apparently, he was an exemplary prisoner. My dad seems to think William's fatal heart attack last year might have helped nudge the dial more in Ben's favour. That, and prison overcrowding isn't getting any better. Not much sense in keeping a man locked up for attempted murder when the person he was trying to murder died anyway."

"And within a month of him getting out, his sister has been murdered, and he's taken over the factory he always wanted?" Damon popped open the packet of crisps and offered them to Claire first; she gratefully took a small handful. "I don't need to be a detective to connect the dots there. Why is he here and not back behind bars?"

"The police must have reasonable doubt not to charge him." Claire crunched through a few crisps. "Maybe he has a solid alibi for when she was murdered? My dad is trying to call in some favours at the station to get some more information."

"I thought he was retired?"

"He is." Claire shrugged. "We're looking into it."

"Why would you want to do that?"

"Because we saw it happen in the place we've worked for years. Aren't you even a little curious?"

"I'm stressed, that's what I am."

"Me too, but it's scratching away at the back of my mind." Claire tucked the article back into her bag, noticing how the stress had affected her chewed-down fingernails. "Two motives have already sprung forward, and the police don't seem to be chasing either of them down."

"Maybe they are, and we just can't see it."

"Maybe."

"But you're still going to look into it?" Damon scratched the side of his head, depositing cheese dust into his dark sideburns. "What are you even going to do? Interrogate and threaten people until someone confesses something to you?"

Claire chuckled. "I'm going to keep my ear to the ground and my eyes open, that's all. If I see or hear something, I'll tell my dad, and he will give me his professional opinion. I doubt anything will come of it, but I can try, at the very least, for the sake of all our jobs. Do you feel secure working under Ben?"

"Not really, but we don't have a lot to work on, do we?" Damon shrugged. "Still think you're barking mad, though."

As they finished their lunch on the wall, the conversation drifted from the murder to *Doctor Who*, as it often did with Damon. Claire had only caught the odd episode of the show when it happened to be on the telly, but at this point, she was sure she knew more about it than most dedicated fans. She almost didn't want to cut him off during his passionate rant about why the companions were being mismanaged by the current showrunner until she realised they only had a few minutes to get back to work.

Once they were back inside, it was obvious they had missed something by leaving the factory. A crowd had gathered at the foot of the central stairwell, and when it parted slightly, Claire spotted her Uncle Pat next to Abdul Hussain. Her mouth dried out immediately; she hadn't thought about Abdul's son, Bilal, once since Nicola's death.

"Surprised to see him back here, considering everything that happened," Damon whispered as they walked to the locker room on the other side of the factory. "Poor fella."

Poor fella indeed, thought Claire.

Abdul, one of Pat's closest friends, had been a shift manager at the factory almost as long as Pat – not that he had been seen anywhere near it lately; Bilal's death had seen to that. Claire couldn't think of any good way to die except maybe drifting off unawares in her sleep, but what had happened to Bilal sent a shiver down her spine every time it crossed her mind.

Claire put her half-finished salad back in her locker. She glanced down the long row of beat-up lockers, eyes landing on the one that once belonged to Bilal. One of the newcomers had taken it over, but she still thought of Bilal whenever she glanced that way.

At first, people had assumed Bilal's fall from the metal walkway into one of the vats of boiling wax was nothing more than a tragic accident. The note found in his locker, along with the diagnosis of depression he received after his marriage broke down, pushed the police to rule the death as an unfortunate suicide.

Abdul didn't believe the ruling, and he never tried to hide it. He even went as far as pointing the finger at Nicola. Some employees were on Abdul's side, but most found the concept of suicide easier to swallow than Abdul's ideas about some kind of elaborate conspiracy cover-up.

"Did you believe it?" Damon asked after shutting up his locker. "The suicide thing?"

"I don't know."

"Me neither." Damon glanced at what had been Bilal's locker. "Never really knew the guy, not really. It's hard to know everyone in a place this big. He always seemed nice. Wasn't the same after his wife left him, though, was he?"

"I didn't notice."

"Me neither, but that's what they said."

After Bilal's death, a wave of concern about employee mental health swept through the factory. Everyone promised they would help each other, even if it was just providing someone to talk to. Something so unfortunate wouldn't happen again. Uncle Pat even set up a lunchtime support group. Pat and Abdul were friends and always had been. The support group was Pat's way of honouring Bilal – but even that faded away. People stopped turning up to the meetings, and life continued on just as it always had.

Clock in.

Head down.

Work hard.

Go home.

Claire couldn't remember the last time Bilal had crossed her mind before seeing Abdul just now, and it bothered her.

Back in the factory, the whir of the machines started up again. She slammed her locker door shut, not really ready to get back to work but knowing she didn't have a choice. She made a mental promise to do better work on this side of lunch, but first, she needed to use the bathroom.

The smell of thick, heavy cigarette smoke hit her immediately. With only one closed door, Claire knew without knocking who sat behind it. Despite the law and the company rules, only one person continued to disobey the no-smoking rule. Today, she wasn't only smoking, she was crying.

"Belinda?" Claire whispered, knocking gently on the stall door. "Everything okay in there?"

The crying stopped, and the toilet flushed. Belinda emerged, wafting smoke from her face, the cigarette already gone. She stepped out and clung to one of the sinks in front of the streaky mirror, her gaze fixed on her reflection's swollen eyes. The crack right down the middle of the mirror split Belinda's face in two, warping her features like a Picasso painting.

"It's Jeff," she said, her bottom lip wobbling. "He's gone missing."

"Missing?"

"Haven't seen him for days," she said. "By the looks of his drawers, I think he's taken some clothes with him. I think ... I think he's left me."

Belinda crumbled against the sink. It took all Claire's effort to stop the heavyset woman hitting the floor. Claire guided her back into the stall and knocked the seat down. She sat Belinda on the lid; Belinda scrambled straight for her packet of cigarettes again.

"Heard a rumour Nicola had stuck a secret camera in here to try and catch whoever was smoking," she mumbled through the cigarette in her mouth. "Can't I have a little crutch to get me through these shifts? I don't want to have to go outside every time I need a little pick me up. It's not right, is it?"

Claire didn't say anything. People had been complaining to Nicola about the constant smell of smoke in the women's toilets. She hadn't been one of them – she liked Belinda too much to get her in trouble — but she hated the scent as much as everyone else did.

"Do you really think he's left you?" Claire asked,

running a soothing hand back and forth across Belinda's shoulders.

"He must have." The smoke drifted up from her flared nostrils, and her eyes fixed on the light in the ceiling. "I think he was having it off with Nicola. Police interviewed him three times. He told me it was routine, but I've suspected something for a while. He's been coming home smelling like cheap perfume for months. Maybe years. I don't know. I stopped paying attention."

"Oh, Belinda."

"It's my own fault." She forced a laugh, tipping the ash from the cigarette onto the top of the plastic toilet roll holder. "I've let myself go, haven't I? I used to be so put together. I eat too much. I smoke too much. I drink too much. I wouldn't want to be with me either. I've been with Jeff for years. I should have known he couldn't ignore my sorry state forever."

"You're not a state."

"I appreciate the effort," she said, smiling wanly as she sucked harder on the cigarette, "but it's a lie. I should probably tell the police what I think. It puts him in the frame, doesn't it? He pushed her and then fled. I don't know for certain that he was even having an affair with Nicola. Maybe I'm just paranoid?"

Claire continued to rub Belinda's shoulders, not wanting to confirm or deny. It wasn't her place to tell Belinda her suspicions were rather spot on.

"That's why I was so cagey when you talked to me outside the pub last night," Belinda continued, stubbing out the cigarette by dragging it along the scorch marks on the stall's wall. "He's done this before. Taken flight for a few days and then come back without really explaining himself. I stopped asking where he'd been. But it's never been like this. And with everything else going on. Should I go to the police? Report him as missing? Tell them what I think?"

"I – I don't know."

"Yeah, me neither." Belinda pulled herself up off the toilet. "I think I need to go home. Do you think anyone will notice?"

"Today?" Claire stepped out of the cubicle. "I don't think so."

"I'll call a taxi." Belinda dug her phone out of her pocket. "I can't face the thought of walking all the way home right now."

"I'll wait with you."

Claire clocked back in before walking Belinda out to the front of the factory. She didn't make a habit of trying to cheat the system, but considering how Ben and Graham were still going at it in the office, she didn't feel a shred of guilt.

"I'll clock you out at the end of the day," Claire said to Belinda when the taxi finally pulled up at the front gates. "You have my number if you need me for anything."

"Thank you, Claire." They shared a quick hug. "You're a good girl."

Claire lingered by the gates and waited until the taxi vanished around the bend in the lane before turning back to the factory. Sticking labels onto mason jars was the last thing she wanted to do right now, but for the sake of keeping her job, she decided against hopping over the wall and running through Ian's farm to discuss her latest findings with her father; that could wait.

She'd taken only three steps before the slamming of a heavy metal door around the left side of the factory made her jump. She detoured towards the sound, surprised to see someone stomping down the fire escape. It took Claire a second to figure out where the door opened on the other side, but after checking the windows, it could only have been in one of the rooms connected to Nicola's, or rather Ben's, office.

One mystery solved.

Claire's father had wondered how Nicola's murderer could have fled the factory without passing everyone below. She had forgotten all about the disused intricate system of fire escape staircases around the sides of the building.

As he reached the bottom, she recognised Graham, Nicola's husband, and her parents' next-door neighbour. To Claire, Nicola had always seemed glamorous and rather snobbish, and she'd thought Graham looked too square for his late wife. He was short, skinny, balding, and cared far too much about bird watching and gardening for a man in his early forties.

The rage twisting his expression as he marched across the car park to his silver Ford Focus, startled her; she had never seen him angry before. He was usually so placid, always with a smile and wave for his neighbours – unlike his late wife. Today, however, he walked right past Claire without giving her a second look.

Returning to work, Claire wondered if it was possible Graham could have been in the factory on the afternoon of Nicola's murder. It wasn't difficult for Claire to conjure up an image of Graham sneaking up the fire escape and catching his wife kissing Jeff.

Adultery, according to her father, was one of the most common motives for impulsive murder, and nothing screamed impulsive more than being pushed through a window from a great height.

One motive. Three suspects. Three angles.

Graham.

Jeff.

Belinda.

CHAPTER SIX

William Warton had always kept things simple at the factory. Everyone worked nine to five, Monday to Friday. As repetitive as it was, it was reliable. No one ever needed to check the rotas because nothing ever changed. The whispering about cutbacks started before his body was even in the ground.

"Nicola's been the accountant here for years," the gossips said. "She cares about the numbers, not our lives."

On a rainy Monday at the back end of the previous year, a heart attack killed William while he sat at his desk. The doors of the factory remained closed until the following Monday. Everyone expected sweeping changes from the moment Nicola appeared for her first shift as boss, but nothing changed.

"Maybe she's not so bad?"

"Things work fine as they are, don't they?"

"No point rocking a steady boat, right?"

For the first two weeks, things stayed as they had always been – but then the dreaded Friday afternoon came. Nicola descended the metal stairs as everyone was about to pack up for the week. She stood halfway up, and in her calmest voice, announced she was cutting the five-day workweek to a four-day workweek.

"It means more flexibility," she had said, looking around but making no eye contact. "You'll have more time during the week to do the things you enjoy, and there will be opportunities for overtime."

William treated his employees like his neighbours, his family. Nobody was ever scared to knock on his office door. In fact, he preferred if you just walked in without bothering with the formality.

If you needed time off for an appointment, you got it. If you needed an advance every few months, you got it. If you had ideas about how things could be run better, he wanted to hear them.

That all ended with Nicola. They were forced to sign zero-hours contracts. Hours were slashed. The workload increased. A handful walked out. Most couldn't afford to.

That's when people started referring to her as the Warton Witch.

"It's just the way things are now," Nicola would say if

anyone dared complain. "The world of work has changed. Get used to it."

And somehow, they did. Checking the rotas every second Sunday became a habit. The group chat was set up so people could swap shifts if they were forced to work a Saturday, and they couldn't arrange childcare. Without a boss to look out for them, they looked out for each other. Things settled into a new rhythm, and even though everyone had less money, they stuck together.

Nicola's murder changed everything all over again. When Ben turned up in his dapper suit and smarmy smile after a week of uncertainty, some of the talk in the group chat after his pub performance was hopeful.

"Maybe he'll put things back to how they used to be?"

"Things can't get any worse, can they?"

The rest remained silent. Nobody wanted to be the one to say Ben was going to make things worse, but after the disastrous first shift, how could things not be getting worse? On Sunday night, the factory phone system sent a text message to all employees.

New rotas online now. Effective immediately.

Nicola's changes had been like swallowing sand. Ben's changes, on the other hand, were more like trying to swallow knives sideways. The four-day workweek had been slashed to three, with some only getting two shifts for the whole week. The shifts had turned from eight hours to twelve.

"How can I afford my rent now?"

"How can I afford my mortgage with these hours?"

"How can I pay for my childcare?"

"How is this fair?"

"How is this legal?"

Claire couldn't remember the last time she hadn't worked on a Monday morning outside of bank holidays, but standing outside the empty tearoom in the quiet village square, her hours slashed like everyone else's, she was glad not to be there today. Some had tried to incite protests, but Claire knew the people she worked with better than that.

Few could risk being fired now, of all times. They would keep their heads down and work. The atmosphere would be foul, but they'd put up and shut up. After all, they had signed Nicola's new contracts.

Claire pulled away from the empty tearoom, unable to torture herself for another second. She glanced at the 'TO LET' sign poking out from the old stone wall, knowing it could come down at any time.

Would someone open a new tearoom? Or perhaps a sandwich shop? Or maybe the candle shop of Claire's dreams under someone else's management?

What a cruel twist of fate that would be.

The empty tearoom was one of five shops on the row. Brown's Butchers was on the right-hand corner, with Wilson's Green Grocers next door. Jane's Tearoom had been right in the middle of the row, with The Abbey Friar fish and chips shop to its left. Northash Post Office, which happened to be where her mother had worked coming up on forty years, completed the row on the left corner.

Once simply a post office, the decline in traditional mail had forced the business to adapt. It was now more of a convenience corner shop that happened to have a small post office counter in it. It was the only place in the village where you could send a letter, cash in your pension, and buy a newspaper, a pint of milk, and a bar of chocolate all in one go.

Chocolate.

Chocolate would help.

Claire walked into the post office. There used to be a single long counter for four workers on the far wall, with an area for organised queuing in neat lines taking up the rest of the space. Now it had two separate counters, one for the shop and one for the post office.

Four decades at the shop had seen Janet promoted to manager, not that she seemed to do much. Even in a rural village like Northash, few people sent letters these days. She'd serve the odd customers sending back ill-fitting clothes bought online and help fill out passport forms, but she usually spent her days reading newspapers and barking orders at the one other staff member of the day.

Jessica Kent, the fresh out of college eighteen-year-old, had only lasted three months, and now they were onto Leo Wilkinson, a twenty-two-year-old with a nervous disposition and mild acne.

"Hello, Claire," Leo said, his cheeks blushing maroon. "Having a nice day, Claire?"

"Splendid."

"Shouldn't you be at work?" Behind the plastic window of her separate post office booth, Janet snapped shut the latest issue of the *Northash Observer*. "Don't tell me you're bunking off, dear."

"I'm not fourteen anymore."

"The trouble we had with you!" Janet pulled off her chained reading glasses. "You and Sally did a disappearing act every P.E. lesson for five years straight. I'm surprised they didn't expel you."

"I'm allergic to exercise, remember?" Claire walked straight up to the row of shiny foil-wrapped chocolate bars. "And before you say anything, yes, I'm buying chocolate, and no, you can't stop me."

"Why would I say anything, dear?" Janet re-opened the newspaper, brows raised halfway up her forehead. "It's your life, or so you keep telling me. I worry about you, that's all."

Claire spotted Nicola's unsmiling face on the cover of the latest issue of the *Northash Observer* when her mother folded the paper in half to continue her reading. Rather than a dramatic headline relying on alliteration and shock, they'd simply gone for:

Nicola Warton
January 23rd, 1980 – March 24th, 2020

Claire had read the article beginning to end that morning over her corn flakes, but there wasn't much to learn. Nicola grew up wealthy; studied mathematics at Oxford University, where she met Graham; moved back to Northash to work at the factory; married Graham; took over the factory when her father died; and was murdered. She had no children and, outside the family business, did nothing all that extraordinary with her life.

And yet, the paper had tried their very best to make Nicola sound like a beloved local hero. Funnily enough, they'd included no quotes from anyone who worked at the factory under her leadership.

Claire wondered how Graham would feel at seeing the paper ignore her married name. She had technically been Nicola Hawkins for two decades, and yet people had referred to her as Nicola Warton as much in life as death. Graham hadn't provided a quote for the article either, although it was said that he was asked and refused.

The journalist speculated that 'the poor man was too stricken with grief to talk owing to the tragic nature of his dear wife's death.' He hadn't been too stricken with grief not to spend most of Friday arguing with Ben Warton in the office his 'dear wife' had been pushed from.

Ben's trial and prison sentence were mentioned in passing, but it felt like they were trying to add extra column inches to the already bloated issue by the time his name came up.

The article ended with a quote from Detective Inspector Harry Ramsbottom's promise that the police were 'dedicated to catching Nicola's callous killer' and 'exploring many promising leads.' They expected 'an arrest very soon' but refused to comment or speculate any further.

Claire knew it meant they were no closer to figuring things out than she was.

"Glenda's daughter joined that new slimming group at the church hall." Janet flipped the page. "She's lost a stone already. Got a little award for it and everything."

Claire ignored her mother and turned her attention to the chocolate.

Dairy Milk or Galaxy?

Or both?

"Apparently, according to Glenda, you don't have to cut anything out either," Janet continued, glancing at Claire over the top of her reading glasses. "It's all about colours and points. Glenda's daughter said it's really easy."

"Good for Glenda's daughter."

The bell above the door rang, and a little girl with plaited, sandy-blonde braids, wearing a yellow summer dress walked in. She scanned the shop before joining Claire at the chocolate.

"And there's that gym across the square," Janet continued. "They've got an offer at the moment, just for ladies. Ten quid a month for the first three months. That's quite a good deal, don't you think, Claire?"

Claire went for the Galaxy but diverted to the Dairy Milk on the way. She almost turned it over to scan the nutritional information, but her mood was too low to know how many calories she was about to eat. Only sugar-rush-induced dopamine would help now, as temporary as it would be.

"A moment on the lips, a—"

"A lifetime on the hips," Claire cut in, slapping the bar down on the counter in front of Leo. "Right now, Mother, I'd staple twelve bars of chocolate to each hip if it helped me feel better."

Leo laughed and snorted. Through the wall separating the post office counter from the shop counter, she felt her mother's lips purse.

"You're funny, Claire." Leo punched buttons on the till. "I think you look lovely as you are, Claire."

"Thank you, Leo." Claire leaned back and nodded at her mother. "Hear that? Leo thinks I look lovely as I am."

"I'm only saying, dear."

"You're always 'only saying.'" Claire dug around in her purse to pull together her small change. "For once in your life, give me a break about my weight. My life is falling apart before my eyes, and being fat or thin has nothing to do with it."

"I'm only saying."

Claire passed over the handful of change, most of them coppers. If things continued on as they were, she couldn't afford to be dipping into her bank account for chocolate.

"You're twenty pence short, Claire," Leo whispered after counting. "Don't worry, I'll let you off, Claire."

"No, it's all right." She dug around in her purse for more change. "I'm not worth losing your job over."

"It's only twenty pence, Claire."

"She's fired people for less." She handed over the money with a grateful smile. "Thank you, though. You're a nice kid."

Too nice to work in the post office.

Most people's spirits were crushed in the first few months working next to Janet, but Leo's smile never seemed to falter. The naivety of youth? Or was he one of those people who always had a smile on their face, regardless of the circumstances? Either way, he wouldn't last at the post office much longer.

"I *saw* that!" Claire's mother cried. "Put that *back*!"

Claire turned, shocked to see the pretty young girl with her dress hitched up. She had a t-shirt and shorts on underneath, and half the contents of the chocolate shelves stuffed down her waistband. She paused, a Twix in her fist. She looked from Janet to Claire, and then to the door. As quick as a cat, she sprinted for the exit.

"*Claire!*" Janet cried. "*Stop her!*"

"Mum, I—"

"Go after her!"

Leaving her chocolate behind, Claire jogged to the door, lacking the little girl's speed. She scanned the square, sure the thief would already be long gone. She was surprised when she saw her paused in front of the small gym on the left side of the square. The girl looked back, catching Claire's eyes before running inside.

The gym had been there for a few years, replacing the inactive library. Much to Janet's dismay, Claire had never stepped foot inside until today. From the moment the door closed behind her, she knew she was painfully out of place.

She looked down at the simple, loose-fitting, army-green top she'd thrown on that morning without ironing. It hung nicely off her bust to cover her awkward middle and was long enough to get away with only a pair of thick black leggings for trousers. She was miles away from the tight-fitting outfits of the women bouncing up and down on the machines. Only one woman looked remotely like

Claire, and she looked like she felt as out of place as Claire did.

Luckily, Claire wasn't there to torture herself with the treadmill. She found the little shoplifter bouncing up and down on a yoga ball in the corner, already halfway through the Twix. A similarly aged, fair-haired boy with a full face of freckles sat next to her on an aerobics step, his face buried in a handheld games console.

"C'mon!" Claire said, holding out her hand. "Cough up."

"Go away, lady."

"Excuse me?"

"I said, *go away*!" The girl stuck out her chocolate-coated tongue before taking another bite. "You're not a member."

"I might be."

"You're not." The girl looked her up and down. "And it's members-only in here. You're breaking the rules."

"Says the shoplifter!" Claire forced a laugh, hands planting on her hips. "How old are you?"

"Thirteen."

"Liar," the boy muttered. "She's nine."

"Shut it, Hugo!" The girl elbowed him in the side. "Don't talk to strangers, remember?"

"You're talking to her."

"No, I'm not." She continued to bounce, turning away

from Claire before she shoved the last of the Twix into her mouth. "Want something, Hugo? I got loads."

Claire cleared her throat and met the girls' distant gaze. "The chocolate."

"Go away!"

"Just give it to her, Amelia."

"*Hugo!*" She elbowed him again. "Thanks a lot, you snitch!"

"Amelia, is it?" Claire looked around the gym. "What are you doing here? Is your mother here?"

"Don't have one."

"Yes, we do." Hugo glanced up at Claire. "She left us."

"*Hugo!*"

"What?" The boy shrugged. "It's true."

Claire didn't know what to say. It wasn't that she disliked children, but she had never known how to talk to them. She'd babysat Sally's two girls, Ellie and Aria, on a handful of occasions, and it had never felt natural. On the last occasion, Ellie had been playing with Aria's doll and Aria with Ellie's. They had both wanted their own doll back, but they had also wanted to keep the doll they had. Claire hadn't known what to do, so she pried a doll from each and swapped them over. The screaming that followed had been so relentless, Claire had to call Sally and Paul back from their date night because she couldn't calm them down. Much to Claire's relief, she hadn't been asked to babysit since.

"Give them back," she said sternly, "or I'll call the police."

"No, you won't."

"Yes, I will!"

"Go on then."

"I will."

"Do it."

"I will."

"Do it now."

"Oh, you little—"

"Can I help you?" A man's voice from behind startled Claire. "Everything okay here?"

Claire turned to the man. A typical gym-goer, by the looks of it. He was tall, and he wore a loose-fitting vest that showed his sculpted body through the sagging armholes. Claire had always wondered what it would feel like to be so comfortable with her body that she wouldn't mind casually exposing large parts of it.

"I've got this." Claire reached into her handbag for her phone. "This is nothing the police can't handle."

"Police?"

"This little girl just shoplifted from my mother's post office and won't give the stuff back." Claire tapped 999 onto the phone keypad. "Like I said, I'm sorting it."

"Claire?" The man ducked into her line of sight. "Claire Harris?"

Claire's eyes left the vest and went up to the man's

face. He had sandy hair and freckles like the two children, but she didn't recognise him.

"Do I know you?"

Her finger lifted away from the green call button.

"It's *me*!" A grin spread across his face. "Ryan!"

"Ryan?"

"Ryan Tyler?" He frowned, his grin faltering. "It's not been that long, has it?"

The phone slid from Claire's grip and bounced onto the foam mat. Hugo picked it up and held it out to Claire with a meek smile, to which Amelia rolled her eyes.

"R-Ryan?" Claire accepted the phone and dropped it into her bag, her hands shaking out of control. "I – I didn't recognise you."

Claire searched the man's face for any trace of the boy who'd lived next door for the first eighteen years of her life. The double chin was completely gone; his once-round face was now angular. Well-groomed stubble covered a jaw cut so sharp it looked like it could split a diamond in two. His Kurt Cobain-style hair had been cut close to his head on the sides, with the top slightly longer and held in place with some wax.

But the eyes.

They had a scattering of faint lines around them, but there was no mistaking the apple green eyes Claire had always wished she had in place of her dull brown ones.

"Is it true, Amelia?" Ryan walked up to the girl and held his hand out. "Did you steal from the shop?"

The girl shrugged.

"You still have chocolate around your mouth." His voice was firm. "Hand them over now."

The girl huffed before she hitched her dress up and pulled out the half dozen chocolate bars she had managed to stuff down her shorts before Janet noticed her. She tossed them onto the floor at Claire's feet, rolling her eyes again.

"Apologise."

"Dad!"

"*Apologise!*"

"Sorry," Amelia said, voice practically a whisper. "I was bored."

Ryan squatted down and picked up the chocolate bars, the thick muscles in his thighs straining under his shorts. He sprang up with minimal effort and handed them to Claire, nodding a gesture for them to talk somewhere else.

"I'm really sorry about her," Ryan whispered, glancing over his shoulder as they walked into the free weights section. "She hasn't been the same since we moved back from Spain."

"Spain," Claire stated, remembering with a nod. "You have kids."

"Don't you?"

"No."

"Are you still at the cul-de-sac?"

"I am." She looked down at the chocolate, unsure of what to say. "I should get this lot back to my mum. She'll send out a search party if I take any longer."

Ryan chuckled. "Nothing ever changes around here, does it?"

"Not really."

"It's good to see you, Claire." He rested a heavy hand on her shoulder. "See you around?"

Claire nodded, unable to speak. Before she let the hundred and one questions tumble out of her mouth, she made for the exit, the chocolate cradled in her arm like a baby.

Ryan was back in Northash. Considering everything else going on, Claire had no idea how to process the shock. Hurrying back to the post office, she hoped the pounding in her heart was from the surprise of seeing him, or at least from chasing the little thief, and nothing more.

She had never told Ryan how hopelessly in love with him she'd been.

CHAPTER SEVEN

*L*ater that evening, Claire was more than happy to hurry down the hallway to answer the door. She skipped the greetings and went straight to hugging Granny Greta, who always gave the best hugs.

"That answers my first question," Greta whispered into her ear, still clinging for dear life and rocking side to side. "It's almost insulting to ask how you're doing after everything I've been hearing."

"You have no idea."

"Granny Greta is here now." They pulled away from each other, and Greta cupped Claire's face in her hands. "Despite it all, you're looking well."

"Try telling that to my mother."

"Is she still on at you about your weight?"

"When isn't she?"

"Hmmm." Greta held her at arm's length and looked her up and down; she was the only woman shorter than her that Claire had ever met. "You look like a healthy young woman to me, dear. If my son wasn't married to your mother, I'd have given her a slap a long time ago."

Greta winked before kissing Claire on the cheek. She shrugged off her heavy coat and put it on the hook herself. Grandma Moreen, Claire's mother's mother and a less frequent visitor, always passed her coat to Claire like she was the staff, but not Greta. Even in her eighties, she still did as much for herself as she could.

"What's this I hear about you hounding my granddaughter about her weight again?" Greta walked straight up to Janet, hands on her hips, and glared at her as though there weren't at least ten inches of height difference between them. "She's built like a typical Harris woman. We don't all need to be stretched out like you, dear, but that doesn't mean you get to pass comment. She's the spitting image of me at that age."

"Good evening to you too, Greta." Claire's mother barely turned away from the pot of Bolognese sauce she was stirring. "Can I get you a cup of tea?"

"I know where the kettle is."

While Greta set about making herself a cup of tea, Claire re-joined her father and Uncle Pat at the dining room table on the other side of the kitchen. They shared the same tight smile, more than used to their mother. Whenever they were together, it was hard to deny that they were brothers. Four years separated them, but with the same round faces, wide noses, bald heads, and glasses, they could have passed as twins.

"You'd think they'd have warmed to each other by now," Pat whispered to his older brother. "How long have you been married again?"

"Forty-five years."

"Forty-five too long if you ask me," Greta said as she joined them at the table with her tea, sitting next to Claire; her hand slipped under the table and gripped Claire's, something she'd done since Claire was a child. "Cheek of the woman!"

"I heard that," Janet called over her shoulder.

"I meant you to."

It had been like this for as long as Claire could remember. Janet and Greta had brief periods of peace, but they were never on the same page. They weren't even in the same book. They were in different books of different series written in different centuries in different languages. Claire had always found it odd, especially since Greta could famously talk to anyone about everything, but Janet wasn't included. They'd taken the frosty mother-in-law and daughter-in-law relationship to another level.

"Play nice, you two," Claire's father said, winking at

Janet with the twinkle in his eyes he still had for her; he was immune to their bickering. "Considering what happened at the factory, we should all feel lucky to have our lives tonight. Any of us could go at any time."

"I'll drink to that." Pat lifted his cup of tea in the air. "Trying times, indeed."

"I heard you saw it, dear." Greta squeezed Claire's hand. "How are you sleeping?"

"Badly."

"Shot of whisky before bed will fix that." She winked and patted Claire's hand. "I once saw a poor fella get hit by the number four bus coming across from Downham. 1954, it was, and if I close my eyes, I can still see his head going all the way around as clear as day. Those things never leave you."

Claire didn't need to close her eyes to see Nicola falling from the office window.

"What are the police doing about all this?" Greta asked her eldest son after sipping her tea. "Those quotes in the paper made it sound like they didn't know a thing."

"They don't." Alan sighed. "I don't know how many times I've told Harry not to talk to the press when they don't know anything. It makes them look inadequate."

"If that tumour hadn't taken you out of action, you'd have caught them by now!" Greta let go of Claire's hand and leaned forward, her finger stamping on the table. "You were the best DI this village has ever seen."

"But the tumour *did* take him out of action," Claire's mother said as she started to set the table around them. "Does everyone want garlic bread with their spaghetti Bolognese?"

Greta twisted in her seat and stared up at her.

"You know I don't like Bolognese, Janet."

"I know, Greta."

"Now, now, you two," Alan huffed. "Could you at least pretend to like each other for one night?"

"No," they replied in unison.

Claire couldn't help but laugh, and it didn't take long for her uncle and father to join in. It was the first time she had laughed properly all week.

As was usual on Monday evenings, Claire's mother was the first to finish eating. She excused herself before everyone had finished and retired to the sitting room to get on with her cross-stitching. It wasn't a written rule that she wasn't to be followed, but nobody ever did.

After the dishes were cleared away and loaded into the dishwasher, the lights were dimmed, and the whisky and crystal tumblers came out. Claire usually passed in favour of some wine, but tonight, she needed something stronger to take the edge off. She hadn't been able to think clearly since bumping into Ryan Tyler for the first time in seventeen years.

"So," Greta said as she poured her own generous measure of whisky, "what are you thinking, Alan?"

"About?"

"Don't play silly buggers." Greta took a sip of her drink, barely phased by its strength. "I know you. Retired or not, you're a detective through and through. You've always been the same way. Claire too. And me, for that matter. We're seekers."

"What about me?" Pat asked, arching a brow. "Am I not a seeker?"

"You're more of a leader, dear." Greta reached across the table and patted his hand. "A man of action. You'd be great at leading an army's charge into battle, but your brother would be in the war room figuring out the moves."

"I can't be mad at that." Pat tossed his whisky back in one. "Not that I feel like much of a leader under Ben Warton. I tried talking to him on Saturday, and again today, but he won't give me a minute of his time. Too busy, or so he says. Busy doing what, I don't know. He's going to run that factory to ruin. Sorry about your rota, Claire. I'm not going to let this stand."

"I appreciated the day off." Claire lifted her glass before taking a sip; it burned all the way down in a way that wasn't entirely unpleasant. "It's not like I didn't want to move out of my parents' any time soon."

"I don't know what he's playing at," said Pat. "His father would be turning in his grave if he knew how quickly his two children had betrayed everything he stood for. It's just as well he's not around to see any of this. Poor fella would have died of a broken heart after what happened to Bilal, let alone the rest of the mess that's happened since."

"So, Alan?" Greta prompted. "What are you thinking?"

Claire's father glanced at her. She could tell he was biting his tongue. She'd told him every detail she'd been able to learn so far, not that she'd found much. Whatever she'd imagined investigating to be like, the crucial information she'd hoped for certainly hadn't landed in her lap yet. With each passing day, she was running out of steam.

"I have some theories," Alan started after tossing back the alcohol, his reaction as mute as his mother's. "Claire's got her old man's brain, and she's been listening out. Found some interesting leads, haven't you, Claire, my dear?"

"I wouldn't say that, exactly." Claire felt her cheeks heat, so she forced down more whisky. "Before Nicola fell, I saw her kissing Jeff through the office window."

"Health and Safety Jeff?" asked Pat.

"The very same." Claire tossed back the last of the drink; a warm glow floated through her insides, and she suddenly saw the appeal. "Most days, I work with his wife, Belinda, on the labelling station. Jeff was kissing

Nicola, and Nicola pulled away. That's when I was outside. I went inside a couple of minutes later with Damon, my work friend, and ... well, you know what happened next."

"And you didn't see who pushed her?" Greta asked, topping up Claire's glass. "Well, I'm assuming not, since no one's behind bars."

"If only I'd looked up while she was falling," Claire mused aloud. "Might have seen them. But I was too shocked to think."

"Surely, it was Jeff, then?" Pat reached across the table for the bottle. "If he was kissing Nicola right before?"

"He's the most obvious suspect," Alan agreed. "Police seem to think so, at least, but he's gone AWOL. Hasn't been seen since Thursday, according to his wife. And she seems to know about the affair too, which puts her high up on the list. Do you remember the Johnny Jones case?"

Greta nodded eagerly. "1977. Murdered by his wife, Linda, because she caught him in bed with her sister. Took a kitchen knife to his throat then and there."

"And she would have got the sister, too, if she hadn't jumped through the bedroom window," Alan added. "In her birthday suit, too. Broke both ankles, but the neighbours saw her and took her in. Didn't stop Linda going looking for her, though. Knife in hand, covered in her husband's blood, with a crazed look in her eyes according to eyewitnesses. Swung for the police when they showed up. Said in court she didn't remember any of it."

"Nothing worse than a woman scorned." Greta circled her finger around her tumbler. "Can't say I wouldn't have done the same if I'd caught your father in bed with one of my sisters, God rest his soul."

"So, you think it's the same thing here?" Pat asked.

Alan tipped his head from side to side. "Could be. Seems plausible. But Belinda was in the factory at the time of the murder. Claire saw her there in the morning, and she could have easily gone down the fire escape unseen. Both have motive and opportunity, but Claire doesn't seem to think Belinda could be to blame."

"You two friends?" Greta asked.

"Work friends," Claire corrected. "I like her, but I don't really know her outside of the factory. I don't think she did it, though. She was suspicious about the affair but didn't seem certain. And why would she admit to being suspicious if she'd done it? Unless…"

"Unless?" Pat prompted.

"Well, she'd know who my dad is." Claire looked at her father. "She might not know he's retired. What if she purposefully tried to throw me off the scent?"

Alan smiled proudly. "Now you're thinking like a detective."

"Well, *I* think it was the brother," Pat announced, screwing the lid back on the bottle after topping up his glass. "Ben Warton. He's turned up out of nowhere, taken over, and is somehow doing a *worse* job than his sister!"

"Ben Warton?" Greta's brows scrunched together. "Where do I know that name from?"

"2010," said Alan. "Went down for attempted murder of his father, William. Switched his blood pressure pills for ecstasy and sent the poor guy to the verge of a heart attack."

"That's right." Greta swished her drink around. "I remember now. Wanted to inherit the factory, didn't he? Guess he got what he wanted in the end. Should have just played the long game."

"It's a solid motive." Pat leaned in, his voice lowering. "Fresh out of prison brother kills sister to get the factory he always thought he was owed. It's almost Shakespearian, don't you think?"

"It certainly makes sense." Alan sipped his drink. "There's just one problem."

Claire's ears pricked up. She hadn't heard her father speculate on Ben Warton's possible involvement yet.

"The police will prioritise anyone with a criminal record in a case like this," Alan explained, gaze vanishing into the corner of the room. "Call it discrimination, call it what you like, but criminals are more likely to re-offend. We all know that. Ben Warton would have been pulled in for questioning the very second the police made the connection. I tried asking Harry, but he didn't give much away. Truth be told, I think the man is embarrassed by how little they have to work on."

"So, it can't have been Ben?" Claire prompted. "Because if he was involved, the police would have already found out?"

"Maybe." Alan tipped his head to the side. "That, or he's got a solid alibi."

"And they're not always true," Greta said. "It's not hard to get someone to lie for you if you have something on them. I convinced Mabel from bingo to lie to the police that time they caught me stealing from Marley's Café."

"Mum…" Pat and Alan groaned at the same time.

"It was just a *teaspoon*!" Greta rolled her eyes. "Well, give or take thirty since Jane's Tearoom closed. You know I can't resist slipping them up my sleeve, dear. It was a game I'd play with my dad when I was a girl. Some things stick with you. Marley figured out it was me, so he called the police to scare me."

"He had every right to," Alan said with a chuckle. "How did Mabel lie?"

"Well, Marley had no proof and doesn't have cameras in the café, so I got Mabel to say I was with her for most of the afternoons he claims I stole his spoons." Greta sipped her whisky with a pleased smile. "Wasn't difficult. I'm the only one who knows she wears a wig."

"Not anymore," said Claire.

"Oh, it's fine, dear." Greta patted her hand. "Poor woman passed on last month. Stroke got her in the end. Let's just say her family were shocked when the wig slipped off at the body viewing. She lost her hair through stress in the 1950s, and it never came back. Kept her secret all those years, didn't I?" She drank again. "So, yes. That Ben fella could have faked an alibi, which keeps him in the frame. You have two motives to work with."

"Three," Alan corrected her.

"Bloody hell, Alan!" Pat chuckled, slapping him on the arm. "Anyone else would sit back and enjoy their retirement."

"The credit goes to my daughter."

"Does it?" Claire pushed up her glasses. "What's the third?"

"Well, we have adultery." Alan counted it on his hand. "Then revenge with Ben, and the third, well, it's a little controversial. It's Abdul Hussain."

"*No!*" Pat held up both hands. "I *know* where this is going, and I *won't* hear it!"

"I want to hear it." Greta edged forward in her seat. "Go on, Alan. It's just a theory, after all."

"A *wrong* theory." Pat tossed back his drink, his cheeks darkening. "Abdul is a good friend of mine. He wouldn't do that."

"He has a motive," Alan said firmly. "Reason without

emotion, little brother. I'm looking at this from a logical point of view, and logic dictates the man has a motive. He made no secret of the fact he blamed Nicola for his son's death. And Nicola's fall mirrored what happened to Bilal."

"The wax boy!" Greta fell back into her chair. "Oh, the poor sod! I cried when I heard, and I didn't even know the lad."

They sat in silence for a moment. Domino crept into the kitchen, and when she saw that Janet wasn't around, she jumped up onto the dining room table. She sniffed at Greta's whisky before hopping into Claire's lap and settling; she barely weighed a thing.

"It was suicide," Pat said, his voice low. "Abdul won't admit it, but we all know it was. Poor lad's marriage had just broken down, and he was on antidepressants. Abdul kept that part quiet because it's not as accepted in their culture. It's barely accepted in ours! Bilal struggled to talk about his mental health, and he paid the price for it."

"That part doesn't matter," Alan said coolly, finishing his first tumbler of whisky in a single swallow. "It matters that Abdul blamed Nicola. Whether or not she had any part in it, he convinced himself she did, and sometimes that is enough."

"The man only returned to work on Saturday, and only because *I* called him to come in – we needed the extra hands." Pat drained his second glass. "He was nowhere near the factory on the day Nicola died."

"You know that for certain?" Alan looked at the bottle as though considering a top-up.

"I know Abdul!"

"I think we've had enough for tonight." Alan pushed himself up. "Mum, I re-potted that peace lily for you. I'll go and get it from the shed, and then it's time for bed for me. All this thinking has worn me out."

They usually stayed up close to midnight.

The clock hadn't even struck ten.

While Claire's father retrieved the plant from the shed, Uncle Pat said his goodbyes and left swiftly, his frustrations still hanging heavily in the air. Claire hadn't seen her father and uncle get so heated for a long time, and she hated that it had got to that.

"Don't worry, lass." Greta patted her hand under the table. "As alike as they are, they're very different. Rarely saw eye to eye as boys, but they got better with age. But those old feathers get ruffled up every so often. Only natural with brothers. Pat has always been the more sensitive of the two. He thinks with his heart and your father with his head. They usually balance each other out, but tonight, the heart and head clashed."

Normally merrily drunk on whisky, Granny Greta usually took a taxi home, but after two tiny glasses, she insisted her head was clear enough to walk. When she refused to let Claire order a taxi, she met her halfway and agreed she could walk her home. Despite their earlier prickliness, Greta popped her head into the sitting room to say goodbye to Janet before leaving, as she always did. More often than not, Claire's mother had fallen asleep in front of the television with a wide-open mouth, cross-stitching in her lap; tonight was no exception.

"This is far enough, dear," Greta said when they reached Marley's Café, which cornered the street of terraced cottages leading down to Gary's Mechanics at the end. "Get yourself home. And remember, whatever is going on, you know where I live, and my door is always open."

"Thanks, Gran."

"And my offer is still valid." Greta patted Claire on the hand one last time. "I'll kick that lodger of mine out any time you get sick of living with your parents."

"Things not working out with Terry?"

"Oh, no, dear," Greta said, already walking off into the night with her lily. "I don't think I can take another night of the crying. Most men his age would celebrate if their wife had left them! G'night, love."

"Night, Gran."

Claire waited at the top of the street, watching until Granny Greta disappeared through her front door, three cottages up from the bottom. She smiled, hoping they'd still have at least another decade together. Losing

Grampa George four years ago had been hard. They'd somehow adapted, but she wasn't ready to imagine a life without Greta in it.

Claire turned to set off home, but her smile dropped immediately. A hooded man was standing a few steps ahead under the bright light of the orangey streetlamp. Under the hood, she could just make out his shadowy eyes; it took her a moment to place them.

"Claire, isn't it?" Jeff said, pulling his hood down as he took a step out of the light. "We work together at the factory."

"We do." She gulped. "I know your wife."

"Yeah, you do." Jeff rubbed his hands together and smiled, his eyes on the ground. "Been planting all sorts of seeds in her mind."

"Excuse me?"

Jeff charged forward and pinned Claire up against the wall by the collar of her coat. She landed with a thud, her lower half pressed against the cool stone, her top half against the window of Marley's Café. This close, she could see Jeff hadn't shaved in days. Vodka was hot on his breath. He was a shadow of the sharp-suited health and safety manager she was used to seeing sporadically at the factory.

"Listen, I don't know what your game is, but it ends now." Jeff tightened his grip. "I know you told the police that little lie about me kissing Nicola. That stupid DI slipped up and said your name. Because of that, they won't leave me alone."

"It wasn't a lie."

"Yes, it was." Jeff pushed her so hard against the glass she was sure it would crack. "Now, are you going to retract your statement, or do I have to do something?"

"Like what?" Claire gulped, looking quickly from crazed eye to crazed eye. "Push me through this window? Did you do the same to Nicola?"

Tears suddenly swelled against his lower lashes, and his bottom lip wobbled. And just like that, Claire was sure Jeff had loved Nicola.

"Does Belinda know where you are?" Claire pushed, her confidence growing. "She's worried sick about you, not that she should be. I only told the police what I saw – the truth. And I wasn't the only one to see it. Belinda deserves so much better."

His grip tightened. Tears dribbled pathetically down his bearded cheeks.

"You know nothing."

"I know enough." Claire gritted her jaw. "Now, are you going to let go of me? I'm not going to retract my statement, but I might tell them about you assaulting me."

"Assault?"

"You just slammed me against a wall." Claire looked down at his hands. "You're still holding my jacket, and to be quite honest, you're scaring me."

Jeff's eyes wandered down, and his grip loosened, but before he had a chance to let go of his own accord, a figure ran through the glow of the streetlamp. Heavy hands dragged Jeff off of her, tossing him into the cobbled road like a sack of potatoes. Claire took in the man who had saved her, unable to believe her luck.

"*Ryan?*"

"*Claire?*" Ryan squinted, panting for breath. "What's going on? Are you all right? I was locking up the gym, and I just happened to look over."

Claire exhaled a shaky breath as she straightened her coat, adrenaline coursing through her body. She couldn't remember the last time she had been so aware of her heart beating.

"I'm fine." Claire glanced at Jeff as he scrambled to his feet. "Are you all right?"

Jeff didn't reply. He glared blearily at them both and staggered off, clearly overtaken by his drunkenness. He went in the direction of Greta's cottage but carried on to the mechanics at the bottom before vanishing around the corner.

"Who was that guy?"

"Someone I work with." Claire blinked slowly, trying her best to calm down. "It's a long story. I lied earlier."

"About what?"

"Things aren't the same." She forced a laugh, looking down at her shaky hands. "Not even slightly the same.

Something awful happened at the factory, and I'm somehow caught in the middle of it all."

"Are you talking about the murder?"

"You heard about that?"

"Everyone heard about that." Ryan smiled, revealing familiar dimples in either cheek; the fat might have gone, but Claire could still have taken a nap in them. "Let me walk you home, and you can tell me all about it."

They walked back to the cul-de-sac, and Claire told Ryan every detail of what had happened at the factory. By the time they reached her front door, she felt like she had shed a weight.

"And Nicola lived in my old house?" Ryan ran his fingers across his face, staring at the cottage next door. "You're right, it's not quite as I remember."

"Neither are you," Claire found herself saying. "You've changed so much."

"On the outside, maybe." He winked at her like he always used to. "And on the inside too. It's impossible not to change, isn't it?"

Claire nodded as her mind flooded with questions once again.

"What happened, Ryan?"

"It's a long story." He ran his fingers over his stubble again before checking his watch. "I need to get back to the B&B we're staying at. Jeanie, the owner, said she doesn't mind looking after the kids when I have to work late, but I know she likes to be in bed for eleven."

"You should get home," Claire said, suddenly aware, out of the corner of her eye, that an audience was peeping through the net curtains in the sitting room. "Thank you for turning up when you did. I don't know what he would have done."

"You should tell the police."

"I'll tell my dad. He'll know what to do."

"Is he still a DS?"

"DI, and he had to retire." Claire glanced at her mother, who darted back from the window in a flash. "That's a long story too."

"A drink," Ryan said quickly. "Or coffee. It seems we both have a lot of stories to tell."

"I'd like that."

"Soon." Ryan checked his watch again. "I know where you live, and you know where I'm staying. We'll plan something."

Claire nodded, a lump rising in her throat. She wanted Ryan to give her a date and time then and there, but things were too fresh to push.

"Soon."

"I'll leave you to get to bed." Ryan patted her on the arm before stepping off the doorstep. "Sounds like you've got a crazy shift at the factory tomorrow."

"That's one word for it."

Ryan set off, but he turned back when he reached the garden gate with a smile on his face.

"Mate?" he said, scratching the back of his head. "It *really* is good to see you."

Claire couldn't help but smile.

"Likewise."

Ryan set off into the dark, but Claire couldn't seem to go inside. She was frozen, stuck to the step and leaning against the front door, just like she had been on the day she watched him drive away.

The door opened. She fell into her mother, catching herself on the doorframe.

"Who was that man?" Janet peered into the dark.

"Ryan."

"Ryan, who?"

"Ryan Tyler."

"Next-door Ryan Tyler?" Janet pulled Claire inside, closing and locking the door behind her. "But he used to be fat!"

"And now he's not." Claire kicked off her shoes, shrugged off her jacket, and kissed her mother on the cheek. "I'm off to bed. G'night."

As Claire climbed the stairs to her bedroom with Domino close behind, she hoped the fluttering in her chest was the adrenaline leaving her body and not old feelings awakening. The problem was that overweight or muscular, the Ryan who walked her home was the same boy she remembered.

Once safely inside her bedroom, she took a calming inhale of her last perfect vanilla candle. She lit it and set it on the bedside table, and after feeding the cats some treats and cleaning out their litter tray, she climbed into bed, hoping she would fall asleep easily but old enough to know she wouldn't.

CHAPTER EIGHT

The next morning, Claire climbed out of bed with great reluctance. Her broken sleep had been plagued by bizarre and nonsensical dreams. They all ended the same way: a man standing in the glow of a lamppost, dark gaze fixed on her.

They hadn't all looked like Jeff, and she'd awoken before most of them had a chance to reach her, but one did. Under the stream of the shower, she closed her eyes and saw the face again. With his face inches from hers, wax poured from the man's mouth, nose, and eyes as he pinned her against a wall.

Even though it was impossible, the image unsettled her.

Shaking the disturbing image from her mind, Claire wolfed down a quickly buttered slice of white toast. Her mother didn't comment about Claire's breakfast choice, making her wonder how tired she looked to earn that forbearance. The next twelve hours weren't going to be easy.

Not in the mood to risk being caught by Ian, she walked to work the long way. She followed the path out of the cul-de-sac, almost reaching the village square before turning up past Trinity Community Church. Warton Lane was steep and dotted with sporadic cottages, taking her up the hill to the factory through what many called 'The Canopies' because of how the tall trees created a complete cover over the whole stretch of road in the spring and summer months. When the dense trees broke, the lane levelled out, and the Victorian factory came into view on the hill ahead.

According to the history books, when building began in 1889, Charles Warton chose this exact spot for the factory because it was close enough to the village to walk to on foot, but far enough away that people could have separation from their work. He could have built the factory on any number of spots along the Northash River, leading many over the years to speculate that he chose the spot simply because he wanted to loom over the villagers.

A constant reminder of the power of the Warton family – or so the rumours said. No matter where you were in Northash, you could see the factory, and from the factory, you could see the whole village.

A taxi pulled up by Claire as she walked along the narrow pavement. She ignored it until she realised the driver was dropping someone off and not trying to pick her up. Belinda clambered out of the back seat, somehow managing to look even worse for wear. Claire was surprised she had even turned up for work, considering everything.

"Hope you don't mind," Belinda said, walking behind Claire since the path wasn't wide enough for them to walk side by side. "I could do with the fresh air."

Since they couldn't look at each other much while walking, their conversation was limited to small talk, most of which revolved around the new rota system and Ben's running of the place. According to Belinda, the group chat had done nothing but complain about how Monday's shift was the worst in the factory's history. Even with Abdul back as an extra shift manager, nothing ran smoothly.

"Too few people, too much work," Belinda said when the narrow path ended ahead of the factory's gates. "And Ben is accepting new orders all the time. He seems to think he can cut hours and still increase production. He's going to work us all to death, but at least we have four days off a week, right?"

They reached the factory gates with fifteen minutes to

spare. A few smokers lingered outside, all looking as tired and scared as Claire felt. Perhaps it had never been the best place to work, but such a grey cloud had never before hung over it, despite a bright blue sky.

Usually, Claire wasn't one to linger with the smokers, but Belinda always had a final cigarette before her shift, and Claire felt like Belinda still had something she wanted to say. For that matter, Claire had things of her own to say, or more importantly, ask.

"I think he's left me," Belinda finally said when she'd sucked half the cigarette away. "For real. I reported him to the police as missing on Saturday after I left work. When I woke up this morning, his drawers and wardrobe were empty. Just like that, my marriage is over, and I don't even get to talk to him about it."

"Didn't he wake you packing his bags?"

"I'm a heavy sleeper." She flicked the ash from the end of the cigarette. "The bottle of wine probably didn't help, and neither did the separate bedrooms."

"Separate bedrooms?"

"Jeff's idea." Belinda forced a laugh, lips tight around the cigarette. "Happened a year ago, twenty years into our marriage. Said he'd developed insomnia, and my snoring kept him awake. I barely questioned him; I just went along with it. How long have I been ignoring the obvious, eh? Things haven't been right for years, but I just thought that's what marriage was. I never had a good model. My mum and dad hated each other but stayed together till the bitter end. He drank too much and she smoked too much. And look at me! Their perfect daughter, doing too much of both. I don't blame Jeff. Who would?"

"Don't say that."

"No, it's true." Belinda brushed her wiry, greying hair from her face. "Look at me, Claire. I'm fifty and I look like I'm in my seventies. I've avoided getting close to a mirror for years. I knew what I was doing to myself. Not last night, though. I got right up close to the bathroom mirror and saw the truth. An ugly, old hag looked back at me, and I hated it."

"You're not a hag." Claire rested a hand on Belinda's shoulder. "And looks aren't everything. You can't blame yourself for Jeff straying. That's on him, not you. If he didn't want to be with you, he could have left you without having an affair. He could have been honest."

"I don't even know if he was." Belinda tossed the cigarette and blew out the last of the smoke before leaning against the tall wall surrounding the courtyard. "Nicola is dead and Jeff is gone, and for all I know, he killed her. I hope he did. They deserved each other."

"Do you think he could have?"

"I don't know." Belinda sighed. "The man I married isn't the man I've been living with for the past few years. Jeff used to be sweet, caring. Affectionate, even. We met in 1990. I was working behind the bar in one of those old working men's clubs. I was twenty, and you wouldn't believe it now, but I was quite a looker. Never been thin, but I could turn heads. Vivacious, I think they used to call it. I had the most beautiful chocolate curls. Jeff said he fell in love with me the first time he saw me. Came in with his dad. His first time. There was a comedian on that night. Awful fella. Reggie Smith. Couldn't tell a funny joke to save his life, but he was cheap and got bums in seats. Heard he jumped off a bridge a few years later. Poor guy, if it's true. Gambling debt or something."

With ten minutes to spare before they had to clock in, Belinda pulled out a second cigarette and lit it. More people in blue jumpsuits arrived, most going straight through the gates, a few hanging around for a smoke.

"We dated for ten years," Belinda continued, eyes distant, lips smiling. "Courted, as it was called in those days. We moved in together almost straight away. He needed somewhere to live. I had a flat all to myself. I did all right behind the bar. Hours were decent and the tips were good. Didn't propose until 1999. Never thought he would. Took me by surprise. Wasn't really romantic. He got down on one knee outside the club. It was raining and he pulled the ring out of his shoe. Actually, that does sound quite romantic, doesn't it? Almost like a film."

Claire smiled. "It does."

"We married in December 1999." Belinda held the

cigarette out between two fingers and rested her free arm under her elbow, her gaze still distant. "I always dreamed of a white wedding, and I got it. Bloody freezing, it was, but the pictures were beautiful. We moved to Northash in 2000. New start for a new millennium. Oh, we were all full of such hope back then, weren't we? A new dawn. Tony Blair and New Labour! Things were going to change. But look at the world. It's all gone down the drain. I didn't have any qualifications and couldn't get any bar work here, so I got a job at this factory. A couple of years before you, I think."

"2003."

"I knew you weren't long after." Belinda deeply inhaled the smoke and blew out a long stream. "I wasn't too proud for factory work. When we hit thirty, we thought we'd have a baby. Kept trying, never happened. We never agreed to give up, but we did. By forty, I knew it was hopeless. Should have taken it as a sign. Things were okay until then. I got the menopause quite early. Earlier than most. Maybe that's the reason."

"You can't keep blaming yourself."

"Yeah?" Belinda stubbed out the second cigarette. "I do. Even if he wasn't cheating on me with Nicola, something was going on. Maybe he had a gambling addiction like old Reggie Smith. He could have thrown himself off a bridge too." She paused, looking as though she could cry at any moment. "I don't want to cling onto him. I've got the message loud and clear. I just want to know if he's all right. In the thirty years I've known him, this is the longest I've not seen him. Five days. Doesn't seem a lot, but every day is like a week. *Nobody* has seen him. What if something has happened to him?"

"I saw him," Claire finally revealed. "Last night."

"*What?*" Belinda's tired eyes shot open, and she kicked away from the wall. "When? Where?"

"Outside Marley's Café." Claire ducked her head, unable to look at Belinda. "About twenty past ten. I was walking my gran home."

"We live around the corner from there," Belinda remarked. "Did he say anything?"

"He did."

"What?" Belinda searched her eyes. "Claire, what did he say?"

"Do you really think he could have done it?" Claire asked, glancing up at the sky. "Killed Nicola, I mean?"

"I – I don't know." Belinda grabbed Claire's arms. "Please, tell me what happened. It's written all over your face. What did he do?"

"He pinned me up against a wall."

"What?" Belinda let go. "Why would he do that?"

Claire paused, wondering how best to frame what she needed to say. After ten seconds of silence, she concluded there was no way to sugar coat what was on the tip of her tongue.

"Because I saw him kissing Nicola the morning she was murdered," Claire confessed, eyes on the gravel. "I told the police. That's why they were interviewing him."

A shiny black car with tinted windows roared up the lane, zooming straight through the gates and spraying the smokers with tiny stones. It skidded to a halt inside the courtyard, parking slap bang in the middle. Ben jumped out, shades covering his eyes and a grin already on his face. The car looked new, the glasses looked new, the suit looked new; it turned Claire's stomach.

"Say that again." Belinda closed her eyes. "You saw Jeff kissing Nicola on Tuesday before she was murdered, and you told the police this when?"

"Tuesday."

"One week ago today, exactly?" Belinda nodded slowly, her wiry brows pinched together. "And you waited until *right* now to tell me even after you've seen how worried I've been all week?"

"Belinda, I—"

"No, Claire." She stepped back, eyes hazy with tears. "I thought you were my friend."

Before Claire could explain herself, Belinda doubled back and made for the lane to the village. A couple of the smokers looked at Claire as though waiting for her to explain, but when they realised she wasn't going to, they walked through the factory gates, leaving Claire alone. As she followed them through, she realised why she hadn't told Belinda until now.

She hadn't wanted to see that exact look in her eyes.

CLAIRE HAD HOPED BELINDA'S ACCOUNT OF MONDAY'S horrific shift had been exaggerated, but after only an hour of working at the sticker station with only one other person, she knew Belinda had been softening the blow. The jars flew down at record speed, constantly backing up because they couldn't stick labels on fast enough.

All were wonky; none were rejected. Claire wasn't sure if it was because a quality control team no longer looked over their shoulders, or if everyone had just stopped caring.

When the loud classical music started blasting through the speakers at 10:03 am, it took all Claire's willpower not to drop her work and walk out the front doors, never to return. Her anger only boiled over further when she looked up to the office window and saw Ben sat with his feet up on the desk, eyes glued to what appeared to be a movie on the flat-screen TV attached to the wall.

"He's not even listening to this music," she shouted

over the noise to Natalia, the only other person on the sticker station with her. "He's doing it to mess with us."

"What?" she cried back.

"I said…" Claire pointed up to the office window.

Natalia stopped working altogether to look. She let out a slow laugh as she looked down at her blue jumpsuit.

"This suddenly is not worth it," Natalia cried into Claire's ear. "If I wanted working conditions like this, I would have stayed in Poland. I am sorry, Claire."

"For what?"

Natalia walked away without explaining. Instead of going to the break room or the toilet, she headed straight for the front doors. The music grew even louder, and six more people followed Natalia out of the door.

When the wick-gluing people began screaming at Claire for not being able to stick labels on the jars fast enough, and the wax-pouring people started shouting at her for not sending down enough empty jars, she wondered why she wasn't one of the ones walking out too.

Luckily, just at the moment she was ready to lose it completely, Uncle Pat spotted how much she was struggling and sent one wick-gluer and one wax-pourer to help her. They slapped the stickers on even more wonkily than Claire, but the production line finally started moving again. Not that it mattered much; the new jobs were pouring in on the screen on the wall faster than they could clear them off.

"Break room at lunch," Uncle Pat called into her ear in the brief pause between songs. "Pass it on."

The message spread around the factory like wildfire, and by the time the bell rang for break, everyone had the same knowing look in their eyes. Claire didn't know what Uncle Pat had planned, but she'd heard the word 'strike' muttered more than once.

"*Announcement!*" Ben cried, running down the metal walkway, the orchestral music finally eased. "Listen up, worker bees! We need to up our productivity. Lunch will be cut from an hour to thirty minutes. Don't worry, it's legal; I checked. I don't know what my father was thinking. Who needs an hour to eat?"

When nobody reacted, he shrugged and ran back down the walkway, running his hands along the walls like a hyperactive child. The music turned on as soon as he returned to the office, somehow even louder than before. Thankfully, the canteen had no speakers – not that the door was soundproof. When Claire sat down to eat, she could barely hear herself think.

"At least he won't be able to hear us," Pat called out, standing on a chair like he had in the pub before Ben's not-so-grand entrance. "I think we're all in agreement that Ben Warton is a few sandwiches short of a picnic. I have no idea what that man-child is trying to accomplish, but we're not putting up with this a second longer. No job is worth this treatment. When lunch is over, we stay right here and don't move. We *strike*! He can't fire us all. Raise your hand if you disagree."

Nobody did. From the weary looks on the faces of more than half the people in the room, she gathered this was their second day of Ben's madness. She glanced at the clock; somehow, the shift didn't end for eight more hours. If she had to endure another second of these working conditions, she'd do more than strike.

Unable to hear each other talk without shouting, they ate lunch in silence. Today of all days, she needed her quiet lunch on the wall, but for the first time since Damon had started working at the factory, they weren't on the same shift, and wouldn't be for the rest of the week.

Twenty minutes into their now-reduced lunch break, the music cut off. Moments later, footsteps stomped across metal. Seconds after that, the raised voices began. Despite Pat's insistence on staying in the breakroom to strike, they all hurried to the door. She wondered if this was what had happened after Nicola was pushed, when she'd been on the other side.

Two uniformed police officers were dragging Ben along the walkway while he thrashed like a wild animal. Graham stood in the office, watching from behind the glass, flanked by two middle-aged men in business suits.

"You *can't* do this!" Ben cried.

"Yes, we can," Graham said into a microphone, the speakers carrying his voice through the factory. "Your father left this factory to Nicola under the condition that you would never get your hands on it. I am Nicola's next of kin, not you. I inherit her estate, not you. You're a Warton in name only."

"I am a *Warton!*" Ben thrashed all the way down the stairs. "I am the *last* Warton!"

Even at a distance and from behind the glass, Claire saw the smirk on Graham's face. The two men, lawyers by the looks of it, took turns whispering into Graham's ear. He nodded and lifted the microphone stand up to his mouth again.

"I know you're all still on your break, but this won't take long," he announced. "I apologise for how things have been run since my wife's death. This is not what she would have wanted. This is not what William would have wanted. I am sorry for leaving you to work under this madman. There were a few legal issues to iron out before we could forcibly have him removed. Ben Warton has no legal claim to this factory, and as of this morning, ownership has been transferred to me. The factory will cease production for today. Go home and rest. You will be paid in full for the hours you were supposed to work."

It only took one person to clap for a round of thunderous applause to start. Claire couldn't help but join in, if only out of sheer relief. She clapped for the thought of her bed, which she would be crawling into the second she got home.

"I'd say that's a result," Pat called out, smiling for the first time all day. "You *heard* the man! Get home, get rested, and get ready for him to sort things out."

Pat hurried straight up to the office, but Claire was too tired to linger. She grabbed her jacket from her locker and set off home through Ian's field; facing a farmer with his shotgun couldn't compare to how terrible it had been at the factory.

After forcing her way through the narrow gap in the bushes, she fell into her parents' garden. She spotted Sid and Domino, both alert and looking out from her bedroom. Simply seeing them brought a smile to her face. She glanced through the shed window, glad to see her father inside. Without knocking, she opened the door and was surprised to hear him talking on the house phone.

"Yes," he said. "Okay. Thanks for telling me. Yes, I understand."

He ended the call and tossed the phone onto his workbench, not seeming to care that he'd just dropped it into a pile of soil. He wasn't wearing his work gloves, which meant he'd come out here specifically to talk on the phone – something he'd done often before his retirement.

Knowing it couldn't mean good news, Claire perched on the upturned plant pot.

"That was DI Ramsbottom," he said calmly. "He called to let me know they've just found a body buried in a shallow grave behind the mechanic's shop at the end of your Granny Greta's street. He wanted my advice on something."

Claire's heart dropped to her stomach. The walls of the shed closed in around her.

"Don't worry, it's not your gran."

"Who?"

"Jeff." He inhaled deeply, rubbing at his forehead. "Jeff Lang."

CHAPTER NINE

laire huddled closer to Greta under the golf umbrella behind the police cordon wrapping around Gary's Mechanics. Greta's Yorkshire Terrier, Spud, stood between them, his tiny grey raincoat protecting him from the downpour. It wasn't particularly cold, but the rain had yet to let up since it started that afternoon; it was as if the sky knew what had happened.

It was an hour since sunset, and yet people were still turning up at the crime scene wrapped in raincoats and hidden under brollies. Some speculated loudly; others dabbed at tears; most simply stared.

Claire was in the latter category. Something within her had needed to see it with her own two eyes – not that she could see much. The mechanic's garage blocked much of the view of the place where Jeff had been found, and even if it hadn't, the police had erected white tents to protect the site from the elements. Even with the bright floodlights washing out the darkness, the milling crowd could only make out shadows moving in the tent, deep within the dense forest.

"This is too close for comfort," Greta said, glancing back at her front door. "What is going on in our sleepy little village?"

"I wish I knew," Claire admitted, "but at least we know this wasn't a random attack. Jeff was in the middle of this, and I was starting to think he had to have been behind it all."

"There's nothing saying he didn't push Nicola from that window," Greta pointed out, pulling her raincoat tighter. "If you ask me, I think you should start looking closer to home. That neighbour of yours, Graham. Did he know what his wife was up to behind his back?"

"I haven't figured that out yet."

"Then you know where to go next." Greta handed over the giant umbrella. "You can take this home with you. I'm going to get Spud back. It's time for tea and biscuits, although knowing what happened here, I think I might need something stronger if I'm going to stand a chance of sleeping tonight."

Claire was grateful for the umbrella as it rained all the way home. And not ordinary rain, but the sideways kind that blasted you in the face whether you wore a hood or not.

The rain was so bad, she didn't hear the car driving up behind her until its bright headlights broke through the dense downpour. The lane up to the cul-de-sac was too narrow for two cars to drive up and down at the same time. There were a couple of meeting points up and down the walled-in lane, but cars usually had to fight for their right of way. Luckily, Claire didn't drive, and the cul-de-sac was quiet enough that a huge argument hadn't happened in at least a few months.

Leaning against the wall, umbrella protecting her face, Claire sucked in to let the car pass. She recognised the silver Ford Focus before she recognised the driver.

Instead of passing, Graham pulled up and opened the door for Claire. Without thinking twice, she popped down the umbrella and climbed in. Soaked and shivering, she sat in the passenger seat, teeth chattering while she caught her breath. Graham blasted the heating up to full.

"Nasty out here tonight, isn't it?" he said, easing the car back into first gear before continuing up the lane. "Wasn't too keen on driving back from the factory in this, but it didn't seem like it planned on drying up anytime soon."

"You've been there all this time?"

"Unfortunately, yes." Graham flicked on his full beams,

but they barely broke through the wall of rain. "It appears my dear brother-in-law was on a one-man mission to get the factory shut down as quickly as possible. Everything was a mess. I'm going to have to close up for the rest of the week to figure out the best plan of action. I just don't know the best way to get the message out."

"There's a phone system," Claire admitted. "Nicola set it up. It sends out texts to everyone."

"Oh?"

"I don't know how it works."

"Oh."

"Ben used it," Claire remembered. "There's a group chat. Most people from work are part of that. I could add you, and you could tell everyone yourself."

The dark and tight lane gave way to the lit-up cul-de-sac. Every light in Claire's parents' cottage seemed to be on; Graham's was in complete darkness. He pulled up between the two and killed the engine.

"I'll never get used to coming home to an empty house." His forced smile was melancholy as he glanced at Claire, both hands still on the steering wheel. "Things weren't perfect, but I never realised how different living alone would be."

Things weren't perfect. Did that mean he knew about the affair, or had there been other issues in their marriage?

The question was on the tip of her tongue; she bit it.

As much as she wanted to figure out what was going on, she couldn't bring herself to ask him such a personal question when his expression was so sad. Instead, her mind provided another topic, and this time she couldn't hold back.

"Can I ask you something about Nicola?"

Graham nodded.

"Do you know if she found a little black book?" Claire pushed her wet hair away from her face, the dripping starting to irritate her. "Random, I know, but it was filled with formulas I'd come up with for candles. I misplaced it. Well, I lost it, and I haven't been able to find it."

"And you think Nicola found it?" Graham arched a brow.

"I don't know," she admitted, "but the development team sent around samples of a vanilla candle that smelled scarily accurate to the one I'd just privately developed at home."

"So, you think Nicola stole it?"

"I'm not saying she stole, just—"

"Don't worry," he cut her off, smiling for real this time. "That sounds like something she'd do. If it's anywhere, it'll be in her home office. She was weird about leaving things at the factory. I think she knew it was only a matter of time before her brother tried to get his feet under the table." He ducked to look at the dark cottage, and then at Claire. "We could have a look for it if you like?"

"Only if you're sure?" Claire couldn't believe her luck. "It's not that important."

"It's important enough for you to ask about it." He pulled the keys from the ignition. "It shouldn't take long. I'll even put the kettle on."

In her soggy state, the thought of a hot coffee warmed Claire through. They ran through the rain to Graham's front door. When they stepped into the chilly and dark hallway, Claire realised this was the first she had been in the cottage since the day Ryan left. Nicola and Graham hadn't been the kind of neighbours to invite them over for barbeques – unlike Ryan's mum, Paula, who used any and every excuse to invite the whole cul-de-sac in. Things hadn't been the same since she died.

"There's a towel in the downstairs bathroom," he said as he hurried through the cottage, flicking on lamps. "Get yourself dry before you catch a cold."

Claire shrugged off the heavy raincoat she'd borrowed from her father; she hadn't been able to fasten her mother's. Luckily, it had kept most of her clothes dry from the knee up.

Even though the cottage had an identical layout to all the others in the cul-de-sac, this was the first she'd seen with a downstairs bathroom. It was more a cupboard under the stairs with a toilet and a sink, but a bathroom, nonetheless.

"My mother would have a downstairs bathroom before the end of the week if she knew you had one," Claire called through the door while she dried her hair with the towel.

"That was Nicola's idea," he called back, sounding like he was in the kitchen. "Never saw the point at the time, but it has its uses. Tea or coffee?"

"Coffee."

Suitably dry, Claire left the bathroom. She popped her head in the sitting room, where everything was simpler and more modern than the cottage's exterior would suggest. Paula always adopted a 'more is more' approach to decorating. Seeing it so stark and clinical made it difficult to connect this room with her childhood memories. She and Ryan had always played at Paula's house; she never minded the mess that came with children the same way Janet had.

"Let me know if it's strong enough." Graham handed over the coffee as Claire entered the kitchen. "I'm more of a tea man, but Nicola was a coffee snob, so I expect it's the good stuff. All tastes like ground-up dirt to me, mind. I'm a simple fella at heart."

"You say that like it's a bad thing."

"It started to feel like it." He looked around kitchen, which was even more alien to Claire than the sitting room. "Never really got any of this stuff. I liked it how it was when we first moved in, but Nicola wasn't having any of it. She ... she..."

To Claire's complete shock, Graham doubled over and sobbed into his hands. Ditching her coffee, she hurried over to comfort him, but he recovered as quickly as it started.

"Sorry." He turned to the kitchen window, brushing the tears away. "I'm still coming to terms with what happened."

"There's no shame in crying, Graham."

"Isn't there?" He ran a tea towel roughly against his cheeks. "Only weak men cry, or so Nicola used to say. I was never good enough. Never what she really wanted, I..."

Graham's voice trailed off. He looked horrified at himself for revealing so much.

"I'm sorry." He stiffened up before gulping down tea. "I shouldn't be telling you all this. You don't want to hear it. I'm your boss now, after all."

She offered a smile. "You were my neighbour first."

He returned the smile. "That is true."

"For now, then, it's Claire the neighbour popping around. You'll meet Claire the employee properly when the factory opens again. And Claire the neighbour is happy to lend a sympathetic ear."

For a moment, they sipped their drinks in silence, and

Claire almost forgot why she was there. To look for the book, yes, but more importantly, to figure out what – if anything – Graham knew about the affair. After seeing him cry, she wanted to rule him out, to not suspect him. But her father's words to her uncle popped into her mind; use your head, not your heart.

"We are neighbours," Graham said, as though realising it for the first time. "Neighbour to neighbour, can I give you some advice?"

Sipping the coffee, Claire nodded; he was right, it was excellent.

"You might want to start looking for a new job." He paused to sip his tea. "I'm not sure if I can pull the factory back from where it is."

"Ben did that much damage so quickly?"

"Not quite." He looked down and offered a tight smile, giving Claire the impression there was more to the story than anyone else knew. "You can't tell people this, okay?"

Claire nodded that she wouldn't.

"The factory has been in a bad way for a long time," he said, leaning against the sink with his tea hugged to his chest. "I loved William. I never had a dad; he died when I was a baby. William came as close to being my dad as anyone ever will. Sometimes, I think I liked him more than I liked Nicola. He looked out for me and never asked for anything in return. Nicola used to hate it, truth be told. She was a cold woman. She kept her distance from

139

everyone. I never really knew what she was thinking, and I don't think her dad did either." He paused. "William cared about his employees more than any boss I've ever seen. He tried his best to put them first, even when the money wasn't great. Towards the end, the profit margins were squeezed so tight the factory was close to shutting its doors. Closer than anyone wanted to admit."

"I had no idea."

"That's how William wanted it." He exhaled, staring down into his tea. "He was too much of a good guy to scare all of you like that. He was holding out for some big orders. That's all he needed, he'd say. A couple of big orders and everything would be fine. But they never came. The regular orders kept things skimming along, but these days, so much is produced overseas for half the price, and the Warton brand candles don't sell like they used to. People prefer the handmade stuff these days, and I can't say I blame them. William kept cutting back the fragrance oils because they cost too much, to the point where the candles barely had a scent."

"I noticed."

"As did the shops stocking them. What do they call that? A false economy?" He drank deeply. "When Nicola took over, she had no choice but to change things. I know people thought she was cruel for cruelty's sake, but it came down to cutting hours or laying people off. She would have done either, to be honest, but I convinced her to cut hours instead of making people redundant. Her father would have hated that." He sighed, shaking his head. "I'm not sure if I can fix things with the way they stand. I'm an accountant, not a miracle worker. I might have to sell the factory after all."

"So, that was true?" Claire's stomach knotted. "Ben told everyone Nicola was going to sell the factory. I didn't know if I could believe anything he said."

"Unfortunately, yes; in that, at least, he was honest."

"To whom?"

"A developer." He sighed again. "A property developer. Nicola applied for permission from the council to turn it into luxury apartments and they granted it. The offers lined up right away."

The walls melted around Claire like a candle stood too near the fireplace. She gripped the coffee cup, her fingers shaking beyond control. No matter what she did – even if she solved the murder – she and everyone else at the factory could lose their jobs in favour of apartments they would never be able to afford.

"Let's have a look for that book," Graham said quickly, as though he could feel Claire's panic. "Like I said, if it's anywhere, it'll be in Nicola's office."

Ditching their drinks, they went upstairs. Nicola's office happened to be the same room on the floorplan as Claire's bedroom next door; it was also the bedroom Ryan used to occupy. This room held no bed or candle-making dressing table, just a huge desk in the middle, facing away from the windows; filing cabinets; and bookcases. Claire walked right in, but Graham lingered by the door, not stepping over the carpet separator.

"I haven't been in here since…" He gulped. "Since it happened."

Claire was about to suggest they leave it for another day, but there it was, open on the desk: her little black book.

"Well, that solves one mystery." Claire picked it up and held it tight to her chest. "How I've missed this. I can't believe I lost it."

"Oh, *that* black book?" Graham scratched the side of his head. "Nicola found that in the street. She said she didn't know where it had come from but joked it had been sent from her dad because the formulas were complete and perfect. You did them all?"

"I did." Claire flicked through the note-filled pages; one had been torn out. "Making scents is my passion."

"Why aren't you on the development team?"

"I … I don't know." Claire frowned down at the book, wondering the same. The vanilla page had been taken. "I was put on labels, so on labels I stayed."

"What a waste of your talent."

"When you put it like that…"

"I can't promise a promotion because I don't know if there's a business to open on Monday morning," Graham said, still standing at the door, "but we can talk about it if I figure something out, okay?"

"Okay." Claire tucked the tiny book firmly into her jeans pocket. "Thank you, Graham. I really have missed having this."

For the second time since she'd stepped into his cottage, Graham did something utterly gobsmacking. As she squeezed past him in the doorway, he leaned in close, the scent of stale cigarettes hot on his breath. Closing his eyes, he tried to kiss her, but Claire pulled back, and his lips met thin air.

"I don't know why I did that," he said immediately, stepping back, his expression as horrified as Claire felt.

"I should go."

He wrapped his arms around himself, eyes trained on the floor. "Yeah. Probably for the best."

"Thanks for the coffee."

"No problem."

Heart pounding, Claire hurried down the steps, grabbed her coat, and left. She wasn't sure she breathed until she was safely in the artificial warmth of her parents' hallway. Why had Graham tried to kiss her? Had it come from nowhere? Or was she so out of the romance loop she'd missed the signs? Had she given him signs, albeit unintentionally?

"You all right, love?" her father asked, limping from the kitchen with a cup of tea in one hand and his house cane in the other; he only used that when his foot was really bad. "Look like you've just seen a ghost."

"I was just at Graham's cottage." She pulled the book from her pocket. "Nicola had this after all."

"Oh, that's good!"

"Maybe." She flicked it open to the first page, where she'd very clearly written her name, full address, and phone number. "Graham says she told him she found it on the street. The vanilla page has been ripped out, but it turns out I might be in for a promotion to the development team."

His face lit up.

"Or," she added before he could congratulate her, "I'm about to lose my job. Graham might be selling the factory to a developer."

"He can't do that." Alan limped to the console table in the hallway and put his tea down. "The Warton factory has been there since—"

"1890." Claire closed the book. "And according to him, he can. The council approved it, and Nicola really was shopping around for a buyer. Dad, Graham, he—"

Claire stopped herself. Much as she wanted to tell him about the awkward failed attempt at a kiss, she wasn't sure how her father would react. He was the type of man who would either chuckle it off or go around and bash Graham around the head with his cane for daring to kiss his daughter without her permission; there was no in-between.

"Yes, dear?"

"He—"

But something even stranger than the kiss popped into Claire's mind.

"He didn't mention Jeff's murder," she said, almost to herself. "He didn't bring it up once."

"Are you sure?"

"I'm sure." Claire nodded, her thoughts swirling. "It's all everyone I've seen today has talked about. They only found the body this afternoon, and he didn't mention it, not even in passing."

To Claire's surprise, Alan grinned from ear to ear and rested a hand on her shoulder.

"Now you really are thinking like a detective," he said, patting her on the cheek. "You still committed to figuring this out?"

"More than ever."

CHAPTER TEN

Claire didn't add Graham to the factory group chat. Nevertheless, he found his way in and announced the factory would be closed for the rest of the week. He also confirmed that everyone would get full pay for the shifts they were scheduled to work during those cancelled days. Despite the dozens of questions following this announcement, he left the chat and didn't check in again.

"There are worse ways to spend the day," Damon said the next day, helping himself to another slice of brownie. "In fact, I think this is *the* life. Being paid to sit around eating brownies? Who wouldn't love this?"

"Speak for yourself." Claire took a bite of hers. "I wasn't scheduled to work today, so I'm sitting around eating brownies without being paid."

"Well, I'm being paid." Uncle Pat picked up a brownie and held it to the light. "I'm not sure about all this vegan stuff, though. I miss Jane's Tearoom. Now, she was a woman who knew how to make a flapjack!"

"You really can't tell the difference," Claire's father said, reaching for a second helping from the large plate they'd ordered. "Besides, we'll need the fat if we're going to be using our brains to figure this out." He glanced at Claire and shook his head. "Don't tell your mother. She'll kill us both, and there's been murder enough in this village to last a lifetime."

It had been Claire's idea to meet with Uncle Pat to discuss things. Despite butting heads on their previous meeting, neither brother was the type to sustain a grudge against the other for more than an hour. Since Pat was part of the management team and had worked at the factory longer than anyone Claire knew, she hoped he could provide some insight into Graham on a professional level. Meeting at the café – where they could eat junk in peace – had been Alan's idea. Damon, living above the café, had just happened to already be there, working his way through his second hot chocolate of the day.

"I'm not used to all this sitting around," said Pat after putting the brownie back. "I like to keep busy. I feel idle. No offence, Alan."

"None taken."

"Enjoy it while it lasts," Damon muttered through his final mouthful of brownie. "We'll all be back to work on Monday. Everyone seems to think Graham will put things back how they used to be since he and William were so close."

Claire decided against repeating Graham's warning. Considering both her uncle and best friend had jobs at stake, she didn't want to cause more of a panic than she needed to. She'd warn them, but not here, and not when they had other things to discuss.

"So, Graham?" Alan said, turning to his brother. "What do you think, Pat? Capable of murder?"

"I don't know him all that well, truth be told." Pat picked up a brownie again. "He's always been quiet. In Nicola's shadow, you know. She was the factory's accountant; he did his own thing."

"He did my dad's taxes for the butchers," Damon cut in. "According to my dad, he's a top bloke. Saved him thousands by rearranging things in the business."

"So, he's a wizard with numbers?" Alan wrote down the detail. "Money could be a motive, then? Even if he didn't know about the affair, surely he knew the factory would legally come to him if Nicola was no longer on the scene?"

"He doesn't strike me as money-obsessed," Claire pointed out. "You should have seen his house. Flashy beyond belief, but he didn't seem to care about any of it. He made out like it was all Nicola's idea."

"Maybe he was onto you?" Pat suggested. "Trying to throw you off the scent?"

"Maybe."

"A bird-watching accountant who loves gardening?" Damon circled the empty plate with his finger to swipe up the leftover chocolate crumbs. "Hardly strikes me as a cold-blooded killer."

"Murderers usually don't," Alan said, tapping the pen between his fingers. "I've looked into the eyes of people who have committed murder and couldn't imagine them killing even a spider. Don't let looks fool you. Any of us has the capability to kill, given the right – or wrong – incentive."

"Not me," Pat muttered through his brownie. "I throw up at first sight of blood. Always been that way." He grinned, revealing chocolatey teeth. "These are really good, by the way. You were right. Can't tell the difference."

"But if Graham didn't know about the affair," said Damon, "why would he kill Jeff?"

"We don't know he didn't know," Alan pointed out. "We just don't know if he *did* know."

"This all makes my head hurt," said Pat.

They sat in silence for a moment, contemplating the situation. Claire glanced at the muted TV on the wall in the almost empty café. It was playing an episode of *Cash in the Attic*, the kind of early afternoon television programme she'd have to get used to if Graham really did sell the factory.

"Graham has two motives then," Claire announced when the silence grew uncomfortable. "He could easily have known about the affair. They weren't exactly good at keeping it a secret."

"That's true." Damon nodded. "We saw them snogging through the window. Graham could have seen them. He could have been there, looking through the window like we were. We didn't see him, sure, but we didn't *not* see him. He could have snuck up the fire escape and flipped out."

"All plausible," Alan agreed, his pen scribbling away. "And then he killed Jeff to get him out of the way. Although the rest doesn't make sense."

"The rest?" Claire asked.

"DI Ramsbottom called this morning to fill me in on the details." Alan looked around the café, and when he seemed satisfied they weren't being listened to, he ducked his head slightly and lowered his voice. "Jeff was found in a very shallow grave, which means whoever buried him knew he'd be found. He was hit over the head with a giant rock. Seemed to kill him instantly, according to the experts. They even found the rock there."

A lightbulb flicked above Claire's head. "Doesn't that

mean his murder might not have intended to kill him? If they killed him impulsively, they weren't thinking about getting rid of the body. They did what they could with what they had."

Claire's father smiled proudly.

"Exactly." He stabbed the pen down on the table. "Two impulsive murders, one week apart. Same motive, too, which means we have two likely suspects."

"Graham," Pat said, eyes glazing over, "and Belinda."

"And the other angles?" Claire leaned in closer. "Her brother? And the Abdul thing?"

"For the *last* time," Pat interrupted, sighing, "Abdul had nothing to do with this."

"Well, Ben Warton still could have." Claire stared at the empty plate, a theory forming. "If he killed Nicola to get the factory, maybe it wasn't impulsive at all? What if, and this is just a theory, but what if Jeff saw Ben push Nicola? He was there right before, after all."

"Why wouldn't Jeff tell the police?" Damon asked. "They kept interviewing him."

"Oh, yeah." Claire fell back into her chair. "I don't know. Maybe he was blackmailing Ben? Belinda didn't see him for days. He was clearly trying to get away from the village."

"He was," Alan confirmed. "DI Ramsbottom also told me all of Jeff's clothes were bagged up. Found them less than a hundred metres away, buried in the leaves."

"So, whoever killed him knew he was leaving and tried to hide it?" Claire suggested. "Or at least they hoped nobody would find him that quickly. According to Gran, that's right on a dog walking circuit."

Another heavy silence fell as the quietness of the café swallowed them up. Claire glanced at the counter where Marley was flicking through a magazine. She was glad they were discussing this here. At Jane's Tearoom, Jane would have been trying to eavesdrop on every word, but Marley's quiet, zen personality made him indifferent to furthering the local gossip.

"I know we're all avoiding saying it," Damon said finally, looking around the table, "but Belinda is the most obvious suspect. She was at the factory, and she was clearly angry with Jeff for cheating on her. What did she tell you again, Claire?"

"That when she woke up, all of Jeff's stuff was gone," she repeated. "Separate bedrooms, so she never heard him come and go."

"What if that was all a lie?" Damon's voice sped up: excited, almost. "We don't really know her. She could be an amazing liar."

"She seemed pretty upset when I told her what we saw." Claire cringed at the memory. "That didn't seem put on, but then again…"

The café door burst open, and Marley's husband, Eugene Cropper, hurried in. With his mane of greying hair, thick beard, grand stature, and puffed out chest, Claire always thought he looked like a lion. The brown, crushed velvet suit and creamy cravat only furthered the resemblance today.

"Get the news on, Marley!" he cried, biting his nails as he stared at the TV. "*Cash in the Attic*? Hurry, man!"

"What is it?" Marley slowly closed the magazine and reached for the remote.

"We're on the news!" Eugene could barely hide his grin. "Northash is on the news!"

"We've been on the news all week, dear."

"No, not the *regional* news!" Eugene hurried over and snatched the remote from his husband. "The *national* news! And according to Mrs Beaton, we're the top story!"

"Mrs Beaton says a lot of crazy things," Marley remarked mildly.

But this time, Mrs Beaton was right. When Eugene unmuted the TV and flicked up two channels, the national lunchtime news came on, and there, next to a familiar-looking suited newsreader, were pictures of Jeff and Nicola.

"That top story again," the newsreader stated grimly. "Lancashire Constabulary have confirmed the suspected connection between the seemingly random murders in the small North West village of Northash. According to eyewitness reports and DNA evidence, the victims Jeffrey Lang and Nicola Warton were engaged in an affair before their deaths. Police are now looking for Lang's wife, Belinda, a fifty-year-old local woman who hasn't been seen since the discovery of her husband's body. Local police were reluctant to name Mrs Lang as an official suspect, but they do wish to speak to her as a matter of urgency. Warton's husband, Graham Hawkins, released a statement saying he was 'sickened and saddened' when the police confirmed the news mere hours before the press release. And now, we go to Jake Yarmouth for this afternoon's sport."

Eugene muted the TV the moment the camera cut to the sports reporter. None of them seemed able to speak, so they simply sat in silence, each staring into space.

"Well, I never!" Pat said at last. "I guess that settles it then. The police think Belinda did it."

"They didn't say that," Alan reminded him. "They just want to question her."

"But she's gone missing!" Eugene boomed, his theatrical voice filling the small space as if he imagined himself in the West End's largest theatre. "Surely, that's confirmation of guilt?"

Nobody replied; the silence said enough.

"Closed case, if you ask me." Pat drained his cup of tea and stood. "Which is perfect timing for me since I've a meeting with Graham and the other shift managers to discuss how we move forward. Unlike Ben, he admits he doesn't know what he's doing, and he actually wants our input. Claire, shall I ask about that promotion you mentioned?"

"No," she said quickly, remembering cigarette-scented breath and Graham's ill-advised attempt at a kiss. "Best to wait and see what happens."

Pat left the café, and Claire's father rose soon after. She could tell his foot was hurting him, but he'd never use his cane outside the cottage.

"Do you think it's a closed case, Dad?"

"Not until it's actually closed." He kissed her on the cheek. "Can't afford to get tunnel vision just yet. We've still nothing concrete pointing at anyone. It's all speculation until proven otherwise, and the police haven't enough evidence to lay charges, or they wouldn't have cared about naming Belinda as a suspect on the national news."

Alan left, Eugene following close behind. Marley got back to his magazine; Claire couldn't imagine anyone managing to look *less* interested in the murder. Claire and Damon faced each other, essentially alone in the café.

"Belinda," Damon said, brows scrunched together. "Do you think it could be true?"

"Maybe." Claire inhaled. "Maybe not. Something about all this doesn't feel right."

"I know what you mean."

"I don't think we have all the pieces yet."

"It's not a jigsaw."

"No, but it is a puzzle." Claire stood and pulled her jacket off the back of the chair. "You heard my dad. It's not over until it's over, and until it's over, I'm not pointing the finger at Belinda. I just need to nip to the bathroom, but do you fancy going to the cinema?"

"To watch?"

"Anything." Claire shrugged into her jacket. "I need to not think about this for a few hours. I don't know how my dad did it for so many years."

Leaving Damon to settle the bill with Marley, which he insisted he'd do when they ordered the six brownies since he got a discount for living upstairs, Claire locked herself in the tiny bathroom. She didn't really need to go, but she wanted to check something – without an audience. She pulled her phone from her bag and scrolled to the 'B' contacts.

Belinda Work.

It was a long shot, but if Belinda was suspected of murder, Claire couldn't help thinking she'd want to hear a friendly voice on the phone no matter where she was.

Belinda picked up after three short rings.

"Claire?" came the hissed voice down the phone. "Please tell me that's you."

"It's me."

"Have the police made you call me?"

"No, no." Claire looked around the small bathroom. "I'm alone. You can trust me, which I know means nothing since I didn't tell you about Jeff and Nicola. Please understand I was only trying to protect you. Where are you?"

"I-I don't know." There was a long pause. "A motorway service station somewhere up in Scotland, I think. I've been catching rides with lorry drivers."

"Why?"

"Because the police came for me!" Belinda sounded like she was lighting a cigarette, and the inhale that followed confirmed it. "They were banging on my front door almost the moment I got back from the factory. I didn't know why – and then I checked my phone to find people texting me to say how sorry they were to hear about Jeff. Of course that's why the police were sniffing around at the bottom of my street! I threw up, and then I panicked. I ran out the back. Thank goodness I was dressed."

"Did you—"

"Kill him?" Belinda muttered around the cigarette no doubt clamped between her lips. "Of course not! But I know how this looks. I nicked a fiver out of a woman's pocket and got myself a coffee and a sandwich. It's not my proudest moment, but it was just there. I could have taken more, but I didn't. Saw the bloody news, didn't I! Almost choked on my coronation chicken. I knew they'd try to do this to me."

"Where are you right now?"

"Hiding," Belinda whispered. "In the toilet."

"You can't stay there forever."

"I know that!" Belinda huffed. "Maybe I just need to shave off my hair and hope nobody recognises me. It'll all blow over, won't it?"

"Just come back. They only want to talk to you."

Belinda forced a dry laugh. "Yeah, right. That's not how this works." She sighed. "There's something I didn't tell you, Claire."

Claire waited for Belinda to say something, but it sounded like she was sucking for dear life on the cigarette.

"I hit Jeff," she finally said. "A few weeks ago. I was drunk; I don't even remember it. Again, not my proudest moment. He didn't go to the police, but he went to get stitches. He told them what happened. Police came looking for me then, gave me a warning. He didn't press charges. I swear I have no memory of it, and I know that's not an excuse, but that's not me. You know me, Claire. I'm a good woman, really. I wouldn't do any of what they're saying!"

Claire was about to question if she knew Belinda at all – but there was no denying how many times Belinda had been kind to her over the years, and as recently as the morning of Nicola's murder, when she'd loaned Claire her spare jumpsuit. In all the years they'd worked together, they'd never exchanged cross words until their brief spat outside the factory the morning Jeff was found. Belinda had been erratic, but Claire knew her well enough to know she'd not just committed murder. The way she'd spoken about Jeff had almost brought Claire to tears.

"Claire?" Belinda prompted. "You still there?"

"I believe you."

"You do?"

"I do." Claire rubbed at her forehead, knowing her father wouldn't approve of what she was about to say. "I'll try and help you prove it, but you need to be completely honest with me. Where were you when Jeff was murdered? He must have been murdered in the early hours of Tuesday morning after he confronted me."

Claire waited for a response, but none came. Just as she was about to prompt Belinda, a hitched breath revealed the woman was sobbing as silently as she could on the other end of the phone. Claire let her. When she heard the cigarette lighter flick again, she knew the crying had stopped.

"I told you," Belinda wheezed. "I was passed out in bed."

"Can you prove it?"

"Ask my cat."

"I'll take that as a no then." Claire looked around the bathroom, hoping for a bolt of inspiration. "Wait, where did you say you were when Nicola was killed?"

"Smoking in the bathroom." Belinda chuckled. "Ironic, right? I can't prove that, either!"

"There might be a way."

"Oh?"

"That rumour you heard about the secret bathroom camera?" Claire's heart stomped in her chest. "How seriously did you take it?"

CHAPTER ELEVEN

"You ou want to do *what?*"

"Break into the factory," said Claire, forcing the best 'don't worry about it' smile she could muster. "Well, it's not *technically* breaking in."

Damon scratched the back of his head, glancing down the street at Gary's Mechanics. At some point during the night, the cordon had been pushed back behind the garage, allowing Gary Bushell to open for business. His radio blared, barely drowning out the sound of his machinery. It was almost like everything had gone back to normal; Claire really had to squint to see the crime scene investigators still sniffing around in the forest.

"Claire, you're mental." Damon's cheeks flushed as a police car whizzed past them to the bottom of the street. "Properly mental. Why can't we just go to the cinema like you said? We can be normal. You're going to get us locked up."

"We work there, don't we?"

"For now."

"Then we're just letting ourselves into our place of work, and if anyone catches us, we say we were collecting something important from our lockers." Claire rested her hands on Damon's shoulders and forced his gaze to meet hers. "C'mon, mate. You've got to admit, it's a bit exciting."

"Is it?"

"You know it is." Claire winked. "Everyone thinks Belinda did it."

"*I* think Belinda did it!"

"Well, I don't." She sighed, looking down. "I can't explain why. It's just a feeling."

"Then ignore it."

"I can turn that feeling into proof! If we find the camera, we can prove Belinda was smoking in the toilets when Nicola was pushed."

"*If* we find a camera." Damon fiddled with his glasses, his hands shaking. "It's *just* a rumour."

"It must have come from somewhere."

"Probably Belinda's paranoia!" he cried. "She shouldn't have been smoking in there in the first place, and we all know it. She made that locker room stink! The smoke clings to everything. And for what? Because she couldn't be bothered walking through the factory to smoke outside like everyone else? Or because she knew she was having far too many secret smoke breaks and wanted to disguise them as toilet breaks?"

"Do you want to see an innocent woman get the blame for something she didn't do?"

"No, I don't," he said glumly, "but I don't see why it's our problem."

"It has to be someone's problem."

Damon squirmed on the spot, pouting like a child. She could tell she was getting to him; he'd always been easy to persuade.

"I think I know a way in," he admitted quietly, glancing at the police car outside the garage as DI Ramsbottom struggled out of his tiny Smart car, toupee fluttering in the breeze, "but it won't be easy."

———

CLAIRE HAD LIVED IN NORTHASH HER WHOLE LIFE, BUT even she hadn't ventured into the depths of the forest that surrounded it. When they finally broke through the treeline on top of the factory hill thirty minutes later, she realised why. Roots had tripped her, bushes had scratched her, the streams had soaked her shoes, and thanks to the previous day's downpour, mud caked her jeans up to the calves.

"Exciting, you said?" Damon panted for breath, hands planted on his knees as he looked back at the forest. "I think I'm going to die. Feel my pulse. It's a heart attack, Claire, I'm sure of it."

"You're just unfit," she said, panting just as much. "We both are. Maybe my mum was onto something with the gym membership."

"How *dare* you!" Damon straightened up, sweat dribbling from his thick hair and down his beetroot-hued cheeks. "I'm not fat, I'm fluffy."

"And I'm Kate Moss." Claire cleaned her glasses on the edge of the t-shirt poking out through her jacket before looking up at the factory looming over them. "We made it, that's the main thing."

Sneaking past the police behind Gary's Mechanics would have been impossible, so they'd been forced to follow the pathway down to the canal behind The Hesketh Arms. When they couldn't see the police anymore, they crossed the canal and trekked into the forest, following the steep curve of the hill up to the factory. Though it was the same hill Claire climbed whenever she had to work, it felt less treacherous hiking up a paved road; she'd never complain about the walk again.

"How do you even know about this secret way in?" Claire asked as they set off on the last small section of the hill, which led all the way up to the high back wall of the factory's yard.

"Long story."

"Then give me the short version."

"I was drunk." Damon glanced back at the forest. "That hike didn't seem so bad ten vodkas in."

"Ten?"

"It was my brother's fortieth," he explained. "All my cousins were there. We went on a pub crawl around Manchester. Ended up back in The Hesketh Arms. Theresa and Malcolm stayed open as late as they could, but they turned down my brother's suggestion of an illegal lock-in. You know what lads are like when they get together."

"Never thought of you as a 'lad,'" Claire joked, nudging him with her shoulder. "More of a geek."

"I prefer *nerd*, actually." He nudged her back. "My brother was dead set on hunting down some more drinks. At that point, he would have had white spirits if you'd handed them over in a glass. It was his fortieth, after all."

"Standard."

"I remembered a bottle of brandy I had in my locker," he continued. "Secret Santa. I got Martin the full *Alien* series Blu-ray box set, and he gave me a dusty old bottle of brandy he'd pulled from his drinks cupboard at home. I should never have mentioned it. When my brother gets an idea, it's hard to shake it out of him. He kept calling it 'the mission,' so we came up here to get the bottle. I blame all those years in the army."

"Wasn't he a chef?"

"A chef in the army." Damon chuckled. "Never even went to war, but don't tell him I told you that. Ever since his divorce, he uses the army thing to chat up ladies."

"Does it work?"

"He talks to more women than I do. Somehow 'I work in a candle factory' isn't as appealing."

The hill flattened out and they reached the wall, which was as tall as the two of them combined. Just when Claire thought Damon meant to suggest they climb it, he walked right along the wall until they came to a large chunk of missing stone.

"They think hiding it with the bins means it's not here," Damon muttered as he pushed a giant bin out of the way with his foot. "I only found this because I tripped over and fell flat on my face. Saw right under the bin and through the hole."

When the gap was big enough, he squeezed through on hands and knees. His whole body grazed the stone, but he just fit. Claire copied him, holding her breath against the stench of whatever was rotting in the bin.

"Those are fake." Damon nodded up to the cameras on either side of the back of the factory. "They don't look it, but they are."

"How do you know?"

"Martin, who gave me the brandy? He fitted them on Nicola's orders. Got them off the internet. There wasn't a penny that woman wouldn't try to save if it meant money in her own pocket."

Claire still hadn't told Damon about Graham's warning. They could have been lies or even exaggerations, but she knew they weren't. The factory's financial difficulty was the only thing that had yet to make any sense.

"Damon, there's something I need to te—"

Claire stopped mid-word and they looked at each other, hearing the voice at the same time. Without needing to discuss their plan of action, they ran back to the bin and ducked behind it. The voice grew closer and closer, and even though Claire couldn't see the speaker, she recognised the voice as Graham's.

"I know," she heard him say. "I *know*!"

Remembering what Damon had said about falling over and seeing under the bins, Claire wiggled down onto her stomach with only her hand to separate her cheek from the dirty cobblestones. From this distance, she made out the lower half of Graham's face as he emerged from the left side of the factory. He held a phone to his ear.

"I know!" he repeated. "I'm trying. I know we've waited a long time, but we're going to get what we – yes,

I know. I know! I told you, I'm trying. I'll get the money, just give me more time. You know what's been happening. I know. I *know*! But what do you want me to do? Sell up now? It's going to look suspicious. Of course, I care. Yes, I do. Yes, I love you! Listen, I need to go. Because I'm in a meeting with the shift managers to sort out the mess Ben made. Yes, I know. Of course, I'm still selling, but I need to get things back on track. It could take months. You of all people should know how slow things like this sell. It needs to make money before then, or we'll never get what we want. Okay. Yes. We'll talk later. I love you too."

Damon pulled at Claire's coat, as though to ask what was happening, but she held her hand up. Graham stopped pacing and tucked his phone into his jeans. Both hands vanished up to his face. He leaned against the factory wall, breathing heavily for what felt like a lifetime. When he finally moved, he pulled a packet of cigarettes from his pocket, lit one, and walked back the way he came. Claire counted to a full minute before she dared move.

"He's gone," she whispered. "C'mon."

"Are you crazy?" Damon nodded at the hole in the wall. "We're going back *right* now!"

"We've come this far."

"And we almost got *caught*!"

"But we didn't."

"What has got into you, Claire?" Damon pouted, clearly wanting to dive through the hole; she knew he wouldn't unless she did. "It's almost like you're enjoying this."

Claire gritted her jaw, not wanting her grin to spring forward. As much as she didn't enjoy the reason for her snooping, the snooping itself was thrilling. She'd never truly understood why her father had so loved being a detective, but now she got it. No wonder he was going crazy in his retirement.

"Did you know Graham smoked?" Damon asked, changing the subject. "He didn't strike me as the type."

Claire remembered the attempted kiss; she had detected stale smoke on his breath then.

"I didn't realise I knew until now," she said. "He tried to kiss me."

"*What?*"

"He tried to—"

"I heard *that* part!" he hissed. "When? How?"

"Emphasis on tried," she said quickly. "I went to his house last night to try and get some more information from him. Found my black book there with the vanilla page ripped out, so you were right about that."

"Forget about the candle. Graham tried to kiss you?"

"I was leaving, and it just happened." Claire shrugged. "I pulled away and left, but that's not important. I was trying to tell you something before Graham showed up on the phone, and you've just heard half the story from Graham himself. Nicola was going to sell the factory to property developers to turn this place into flats, and Graham is thinking of doing the same. I didn't understand why he'd want all that money, until now."

"You could figure out what that conversation was about?"

"You couldn't?"

"I'm not psychic, Claire."

"He's obviously having an affair too!" Claire rolled her eyes. "Nicola wasn't the only one. Can't say I'm surprised. The way he talked about her last night, you'd think their marriage never had a happy moment. Seemed he preferred his father-in-law to his wife. You know what that means, don't you?"

"That I need to start looking for another job?"

"Well, yes," she said, "but it means Graham has just given us a third motive for murder. Revenge, money, and now love." She nodded decisively. "Back to the mission."

"You sound like my brother."

"Where's this secret way in?"

Wide-eyed and clearly confused, Damon stared at her like he didn't know the woman he was looking at. Claire wasn't sure she'd recognise that woman herself if she were in front of a mirror. Perhaps Damon was right. Had she gone mad?

"This way," he said with a reluctant sigh.

They walked towards the fire escape door that would take them into the locker room. Unfortunately for them, it only opened from the inside, but that didn't seem to concern Damon. He gathered some strewn plastic crates and created a makeshift stepping ladder up to one of the windows on either side of the fire door. Even from the outside, Claire knew where it led.

"It's been broken for years," he explained as he lifted up the edge of the window with ease. "Been complaining about it for ages, but when does that ever work around here? Not so bad this time of year, but it makes the bathroom freezing in the winter."

Unlike the hole in the wall, the window was big enough to comfortably climb through. Damon went first, and Claire followed, dropping into the men's bathroom. It was identical in size to the women's, but instead of a row of ten cubicles, it only had two, and the rest of the wall was lined with urinals.

"No mirror," Claire remarked, nodding at the bare wall above the sinks.

"You have a mirror?" Damon huffed. "I hate that. Why do people building bathrooms think only women want to look at themselves?"

"I never took you as the vain type."

"I'm not, but even I'd like to know if I have something on my face."

173

"I can be your mirror." Claire scrutinised his face. "You're clean ... for now."

A reluctant smile pricked up the corners of his lips. Despite his lack of enthusiasm for their current adventure, she knew he wouldn't hold it against her.

They left the men's bathroom and crossed the messy shared locker room to the women's bathroom on the other side. The scent of stale cigarette smoke hung thick in the air as if every tile and cubicle door had absorbed the years of Belinda's secret smoking like a giant nicotine patch.

"If you were a secret camera," Claire said, opening each cubicle to check they were alone, "where would you be?"

They scanned the ceiling for secret devices or holes a camera could peek through, but nothing popped out. Her stomach twisted. Had they done all of this for nothing?

"Wait a second," Damon said, staring at the mirror. "What if it's a two-way mirror?"

"The factory is on the other side of that wall."

"Maybe there's a gap?" He pushed his face up against the wall, closed one eye, and attempted to look behind the flat mirror. "Can't see anything."

"There must be a way to detect secret cameras," she thought aloud. "An app, or something."

He arched a brow. "An app?"

"I don't know." She huffed, checking over the middle

cubicle usually favoured by Belinda. "There must be a way. Don't cameras give off radio waves or frequencies or something? You're the geek – *sorry* – nerd. You must know something."

Before Damon could look offended, his face lit up like a light bulb had flipped on in his mind. He pulled his phone from his jeans and opened up the camera. Just when Claire was about to question if he'd joined her in madness, he flicked off the bathroom lights, and a red light, naked to the eye but not the phone, blinked from one of the slots in the tampon and sanitary towel vending machine – another difference between the men's and women's bathrooms.

"That hasn't been restocked for years," Claire said as they walked towards it. The flashing light grew more erratic. "We all make sure we keep that stuff in our lockers – more for the newbies than anything. They see that and think they're covered in emergencies."

Damon rested the camera on the edge of the sink before running his fingers along the edge of the metal vending machine. He landed on the lock in the top left-hand corner, but the front door didn't give.

"It's locked," he said, staring through the narrow gap around the edge with one eye closed. "It's only a simple up and down lock, like the bathroom stalls. If we can find something thin enough to get through that gap, we can shimmy it up."

"I have an idea," Claire said, already walking to the door. "Wait here."

She made her way to the door leading onto the factory floor. There was every possibility that Graham could be directly on the other side. She paused, wondering if she should risk being caught. She'd nearly decided to search the locker room for something ... but she had nothing to lose. If she didn't get to the bottom of the murders soon, there wouldn't be a job to lose.

Luckily for Claire, Graham was up in the office with Uncle Pat, Abdul, and the other two shift managers, Bianca and Oliver. None of them were looking through the window, but she still dropped down to her hands and knees. She shimmed along the old tiles, darting behind machines until she got to the wax-pouring station, where she found six of what she needed; she grabbed one and retraced her steps – or crawl – back to the bathroom.

"Excess wax scraper," she said to Damon when she handed over the flat tool. "Is it thin enough?"

"We'll find out."

Damon slid the tool through the gap. It fit with ease. Usually, it was used to skim the tops of tea light and glass jar candles, scraping off the surplus wax for re-melting. The lock clicked, and the door swung open.

"Wow," Damon remarked, shaking his head. "Maybe you're not going crazy after all."

They stared at the tiny camera. It sat where the

mechanics for the money slot would have been, but the machine had been gutted.

"It's been hooked up to the vending machine power source," Damon said, pointing to the tangled-up wires. "Badly, but it seems to be working. I think it's recording us right now. She must have really wanted to catch that smoker."

"Enough people complained about it," she said. "More than the broken window in the men's, I'm guessing. Where do the videos go?"

Damon yanked out some wires and pulled out the tiny camera. He turned it around and pointed to a small slot.

"Internal memory card," he explained. "The videos will store directly on here and maybe send to a cloud memory for backup, but it should all be on here."

"So, you can see if Belinda was in here when she said she was?"

"There might be an automatic overwrite process to save memory," he said, pocketing the camera. "But if there isn't, I can see. Shouldn't take too long to find either."

"Then let's get out of here." Claire shut the vending machine door. "Before our luck runs out."

They left the factory the way they snuck in, but instead of risking the tricky forest again, they chanced Ian's farm instead. Halfway down the hill, he emerged from his farmhouse, screaming and shouting, forcing them to run the rest of the way to Claire's cottage. Somehow, they both avoided the cow dung.

After she settled Damon in the sitting room with a cup of tea, a generous slice of cake, and a laptop to check the camera, she joined her father in the shed. She told him all about her conversation with Belinda, overhearing Graham, breaking into the factory, and finding the camera. She expected a scolding, but he looked more impressed than anything.

"You're right," he said after considering her theories. "Graham does have three motives, and you may have just found additional evidence without even realising it."

"Oh?"

"The smoking," he said, pulling off his muddy gloves. "While you were hopping walls and playing spy, forensics found something in Jeff's shallow grave. DI Ramsbottom thinks it's probably nothing, and I wasn't sure either, but now it seems too much a coincidence not to be connected."

"What did they find?"

"Chewing gum," he revealed, leaning back in his chair and staring at the cactus from the bathroom he'd transferred to a bigger pot. "Nicotine chewing gum. The kind people use to help them quit smoking."

CHAPTER TWELVE

*C*laire didn't bother setting an alarm before going to sleep that night. Not that she needed to. Her mother woke her bright and early by tossing back the curtains.

"*Why?*" Claire groaned, pulling the covers up over her eyes.

"You need to get up."

"What time is it?"

"Just after eight."

"Leave me alone." Claire rolled over, burying her face in her pillow. "The factory isn't open this week."

"It's not about the factory."

"Then where's the fire?"

"The police are here."

"*What?*" Claire sat up, so violently that she scared

Domino and Sid away from their spots curled up at the bottom of the bed. "Why?"

"They're here to see you."

"Why?"

"They wouldn't tell me," she said, fiddling with her diamond earrings. "Oh, Claire! What have you done?"

"I thought the cameras were fake."

"Cameras?" Her lips pursed. "What cameras?"

Claire rubbed her eyes, hoping she was about to wake up from a horrible dream. Sid meowed as he stalked his empty food bowl, letting her know she was very much awake.

"I broke into the factory yesterday," she said, reluctantly climbing out of bed, still half asleep. "Well, technically, there was no breaking in. We climbed through a broken window."

"We?" She pinched the bridge of her nose. "Who is 'we'? If you tell me your father—"

"Damon." Claire quickly changed out of her pyjama bottoms and into a pair of tight-fitting thick black leggings. "Do you think Dad could climb through a window with his foot?" She pulled a longline blouse from her messy drawers. "Turn around."

"Claire, I've seen you naked a thousand times."

"And all of them before I was old enough to have any say in it." Claire pulled the blouse the right way out, ignoring the million creases. "Turn around."

With a huff and puff, Janet turned, fiddling with her wristwatch. As Claire pulled on a comfy bra under her pyjama top, she wondered how her mother always looked so put together so early in the morning. Did she go to sleep every night fully dressed, hair blow-dried, and make-up lightly applied in case she had to wake up for a fire? Claire couldn't imagine having the energy.

"Right, I'm done." Claire ran a brush through her mousy bob and grabbed her glasses from the bedside table. "Is it DI Ramsbottom?"

Janet shook her head. "An ordinary PC. Michael something or other. Looks young."

"That's a good sign. They'd have sent someone more senior if I was in bad trouble."

"Why in heavens did you break into the factory?"

"To get evidence."

"Is that why Damon was on my laptop yesterday?"

"Nothing to hide, I hope?"

Claire's teasing was met with an even tighter pursing of the lips.

"No," she said. "I was just wondering, that's all. He's not exactly who I'd imagine being the father of my grandchildren, but he's a man, so that's a start."

"Damon is my friend."

"I'm only saying, it would be nice—"

"Nice if I popped out a few grandkids to show off at your Women's Institute meetings?" Claire ran a roll-on under in her armpits through the loose armholes. "Even when there's a police officer downstairs, you don't switch off, do you?"

"I'm only saying." Janet picked a piece of lint off Claire's shoulder. "You're not gay, are you, dear?"

"What?"

"Gay," she repeated. "Like Marley and Eugene."

"You're unbelievable."

"There's nothing wrong with it," she said, her voice feigning all the casualness she could muster. "Not these days."

"And if I was?"

"Then I'd be able to explain you to my friends. You know I'm the—"

"Only one without grandchildren." Claire assessed herself in the mirror; she looked as thrown together as she felt. "Yes, I know. You remind me almost hourly."

"Glenda's daughter, the one who lost all that weight at the new slimming club, she's a ... Oh, what's the politically correct term these days? I can't keep up."

"A lesbian?"

"Yes," she said, pausing to gulp, "a *lesbian*." She joined Claire in the mirror and gave her choice of outfit a scathing glare hidden behind a polite smile. "She's adopted. You can do all sorts these days. If you are a ... lesbian, then I suppose—"

"Mother." Claire rested both hands on Janet's

shoulders. "I don't know how to break it to you, but I'm not a lesbian."

"Then what's the issue?"

"Who says there's an issue."

"You're not getting any—"

"Younger, I know." Claire quickly fed the cats; she'd come back to clean the litter tray later if the PC hadn't carted her off in handcuffs. "Another fact you constantly remind me of. Believe it or not, Mother, there might be more to life than getting married and having children."

"Like what?"

"Following a dream."

"You don't have a dream, Claire." Janet jumped back when both cats ran past her to their food bowls. "What was it all your school reports said? 'Must try harder.'"

Claire didn't know whether to laugh or cry. She knew her mother meant no harm, but even though her voice was as soft and well-spoken as ever, her lack of filter made for abrasive listening after such a rude awakening.

"Mother." Claire rested her hands on Janet's shoulders again. "I love you very much."

"And I love you too, Claire."

"I love you," Claire continued, "but please, put a sock in it, yeah? There's a copper downstairs, and he might be about to arrest me. The last things I want to think about are my weight, lack of a husband, or the expiry date on my reproductive organs. If it's all the same to you, I'd rather get this over with."

"I'm only saying, Claire."

"I know." She patted her mother softly on the cheek. "And I know deep down it's because you care."

"Of course I care," she said, lips pursed again, "but at the end of the day, I just want what's best for—"

Claire rested a finger against her mother's lips.

"You can lecture me as much as you want later, I promise." Claire kissed her on the cheek. "Is Dad still in bed?"

"Hospital for a routine check-up scan."

"Okay." Claire reached for the door handle, her heart pounding in her chest. "I'm sure I'll be fine on my own. If I need a lawyer, we can call Uncle Richard."

"Hmmm." She picked more lint off Claire's blouse. "And, dear, if they're going to arrest you, don't put up a fight. The last thing we need is you making a scene in front of the neighbours."

Claire found the uniformed police constable in the sitting room, dunking one of the laid-out chocolate digestive biscuits into his cup of tea. He looked far too young to be qualified to do anything more strenuous than delivering papers, but that could be her warped view of everyone younger than her since she'd entered her thirties. Somewhere along the way, she'd stopped being able to tell the difference between eighteen-year-olds and twenty-four-year-olds.

"Claire Harris?" he muttered through his mouthful of mushy biscuit, half-standing to greet her. "PC Matthew Cameron."

"Nice to meet you," she lied, perching on the sofa, nervous in her own home.

"Harris," he repeated, a smile pricking the corners of his lips. "No relationship to DI Alan Harris, by any chance?"

"Father."

"Really?" His smile grew. "Never got to work with the fella, but all the boys at the station speak so highly of him. If he's around, I'd love to pick his brains about—"

"He's not," she cut in, her nerves growing. "What's this about?"

"Right." PC Cameron dusted the crumbs off his hands and pulled his small pad from his pocket. "We've had a report of theft from a Mister Graham Hawkins, who I understand is your boss?"

"He is," she confirmed. "Listen, I'll admit to it. I took the camera, but it's only to try and help Belinda."

"Belinda?"

"The woman your boss has plastered all over the news," she said. "Everyone thinks she killed her husband and his mistress, but I don't, and the camera could prove that. We'd have proved it by now, but the files are encrypted and Damon—"

"Damon?" he cut in, not writing a word of it down.

"Damon Gilbert," she said, sinking further into the chair. "We work together. He's working on the files to try and crack them, but—"

"Mrs Harris."

"*Miss*," her mother called from the hallway.

"Miss Harris," he corrected, blushing. "I'm not quite following."

"You're not?"

"I'm not."

A penny dropped deep in Claire's mind; it was her turn to blush. She fidgeted in her seat, wondering if she'd just landed herself in more trouble than needed.

"I haven't had my morning coffee yet," she said, attempting to laugh it off. "May I ask why you're here?"

"Your boss, Graham Hawkins," he started, reading aloud from his pad, "alleges that you stole equipment from your place of work. A thermometer, scales, jugs, stirrers, that sort of thing. Candle-making stuff, he said."

"Oh."

"Does this ring a bell?"

"It does." Claire tried to hold in her sigh of relief. "Yes, I'll admit to taking those things. They're upstairs now if you want to see them. But I didn't steal them. Not really. They're what the development team uses to mix up new small batches, and they were being thrown out to make way for new things, so I took them."

"Did you ask permission first?"

"Well, no, but—"

"Then she was *recycling* them!" Claire's mother barged in. "I don't know what kind of operation you're running here, but you're not going to lock my daughter up and throw away the key over some recycled bits of junk! My brother is a lawyer, you know. It'll only take one phone call and he'll be straight here on the first train from Manchester! What did you say your name was?"

"PC Mathew Cameron."

"Let me see your badge." Janet clicked her fingers and held out her hands. "I know my daughter's rights."

"Mum—"

"No, Claire!" Janet held up a hand. "We might have left the EU, but we still have laws! This isn't Guantanamo Bay!"

PC Cameron smiled at Claire as he pulled out his badge.

"Mrs Harris?" he said, looking at Claire's mother. "I'm not arresting your daughter."

"You're not?" She scanned the badge and passed it back.

"No." He tucked his badge away. "We don't make a habit of arresting people for taking jugs and thermometers from their place of work, but we are obliged to follow up all reports." He turned to Claire. "Today, you'll be let off with a caution for petty theft. It won't show up on a criminal record, but it will be kept in the police's internal database. I'd suggest perhaps returning the items and seeing if you can sort things out with your boss." He paused, inhaling deeply. "And he told me to tell you that you have been fired."

"Fired?" Claire echoed, the word jamming in her throat.

"*Fired?*" Janet shrieked. "She's wasted seventeen years of her life there, and he's firing her over *this*?"

"I'm just the messenger," he said, standing and taking another biscuit. "Thank you for the tea, Mrs Harris. I'll show myself out."

The young PC walked out, leaving behind the aftermath of his bombshell. Claire sank deeper into the sofa as the reality of the situation hit her all at once. Graham would never have called the police if she hadn't rejected his kiss; she felt it deep in her bones.

"We'll fight this," Janet insisted, taking the armchair the officer had been sat in. "I'll call Uncle Richard. He'll know what to do. We'll sue!"

But Claire didn't have the energy to respond. She left the living room, slid her feet into her shoes, and set off into the unknown.

Ever the glutton for punishment, Claire found herself back at the empty shop. The 'TO LET' sign still jutted from the old stone, not that it mattered. The young PC had just dropped an atomic bomb on the last shred of hope she had of her dream ever coming true.

'Must try harder,' her mother had quoted. Had the teachers been right for all those years? Claire always knew she had the capability to do well at school, but for whatever reason, she never put in more than the minimum effort. She wasn't a rebel. Growing up with a DI for a father made it impossible not to respect authority, but she'd never seen the point of school. Her five years at high school had felt like a series of memory games, each new thing forgotten almost as quickly as it had been learned. At the end of it all, she walked out with a sheet of paper littered with Cs in all the subjects that mattered, a B in art, and a D in French. She had yet to find a use for Pythagoras' theorem, had never encountered a French person who didn't also speak English, and had never tried to replicate another artist's work for analysis.

But if she had tried harder, would she be further along? Sally had tried. They'd bunked off P.E. together, but Sally revised her backside off for the exams. She went to college, and university, and became a top estate agent. She had a house, husband, and kids: the full package.

What did Claire have?

A shattered dream and a disappointed mother.

"Penny for your thoughts?" Ryan said, appearing behind her in the reflection of the mirror. "Lusting after Jane's iced buns?"

"What?"

"The tearoom," he said, stuffing his hands into the pockets of his baggy gym shorts. "I still can't believe Jane actually retired. I thought she'd be there until the end of time. You were right. Things do change around here after all."

"I suppose they do."

"You okay, mate?" He ducked to meet her eyes. "You look like you've heard some really bad news."

"I have." She attempted to muster a smile, but it didn't come. "I've just been fired."

"Oh." His pale cheeks flooded red; she always used to love how quickly and easily he blushed. "Sorry, I was messing around."

"It's not your fault." She took one last look at the shop before turning away. "I got myself into this mess."

"How about that coffee?" he suggested, hooking his thumb over his shoulder back to the gym. "I don't start work till half-past, and I still haven't tried that little vegan café."

Claire glanced at her watch.

"I think I need something stronger," she said, already setting off to The Hesketh Arms.

The Hesketh Arms opened at eight every morning for the breakfast rush and started serving alcohol from nine. Luckily for Claire, it was five past nine and the majority of the early morning breakfast rush were already on their way out when they arrived. By the time they settled in a quiet corner with two pints of the Hesketh Homebrew, the pub was almost empty.

"Still tastes the same," Ryan said after a sip. "Remember how we'd get my mum to sneak us the homebrew because we weren't old enough to get served?"

"She'd bring it in a Tupperware box, and we'd share a pint between us."

"How old must we have been?"

"Fifteen?"

"Fifteen." Ryan sucked the air through his teeth. "Where have those twenty years gone?"

Into your abs, Claire thought.

"Do you think you'll find another job?" he asked after a brief silence. "It was never easy around here. I'm lucky I got my personal trainer qualification a few years ago, or I'd have been on the scrapheap with you. Sorry."

"I don't know," she admitted. "I haven't thought that far ahead."

"Living in the moment, eh?"

"It only happened this morning."

"Oh." Ryan gulped down more of this pint. "I'm sorry. This is a bit awkward, isn't it?"

Claire hadn't wanted to admit it to herself, but it was, and she knew she was the one making it awkward. She could barely bring herself to look at him. When she looked away, the voice was the one she remembered, but the face and body belonged to another man entirely. Was she mourning the chubby, round-faced version of Ryan she'd been madly in love with as that teenage girl sharing sips of lager from a plastic tub?

"Sorry," Claire said after a calming sip of beer. "Tell me everything."

"Everything?"

"Everything." She nodded. "Why are you back here? What happened?"

"It's a long story."

"It's a long pint." Claire glanced at the clock on the wall. "And you have twenty minutes before you need to get to work."

Ryan looked down, a smile spreading across his face.

"What?" Claire prompted.

"Nothing," he replied. "I just missed this. You and me. We might be older and wiser, but this feels the same, doesn't it?"

Claire thought about it for a moment. "Yeah, I suppose it does. Although, speak for yourself. I'm no wiser. Still fumbling through life, trying to figure things out."

"Aren't we all?" Ryan sighed. "I never thought I'd be

back here living out of a B&B, about to get divorced, looking after two kids on my own. Starting again at thirty-five certainly wasn't in the life plan, but Maya had other ideas."

Claire's stomach knotted. There it was: the name she had spent seventeen years trying to forget; the name that had broken her heart.

"What happened?" she managed to ask.

"She ran off with the only friend I made while I was living in Spain," he started, his eyes glazing over. "It wasn't easy leaving Northash to start a new life in a new country. I don't know why I thought it would be. Not many people leave their home to risk it all with someone they'd met on a lad's holiday. Looking back, I don't think I would have if Mum hadn't just died."

Claire's stomach knotted again, but for a different reason. Paula, Ryan's mother, came into her thoughts often. Even if she hadn't been friends with Ryan, Paula would have been her favourite neighbour in the cul-de-sac. The cancer had been so aggressive, it had taken her before anyone could wrap their heads around the idea that she was dying.

"Maya helped a lot," he continued after another sip. "She was great, really. Her family became my family. I started taking care of myself. The Spanish eat differently than we do. More salads and fewer chips. The weight melted off me, and then I fell in love with exercise. That's when I met Will. He helped me train, taught me the right way to do things in the gym. He became my best friend. Having that one friend made life out there easier. It wasn't like I had much to come home to."

You had me, Claire thought.

"I'm sorry we lost touch," he said, glancing at her, his head bowed. "It was different back then, wasn't it? No social media. I did try. The phone calls, the letters. Maya didn't like it. She was jealous. She didn't understand what our friendship was, so it was easier just to stop."

"It's fine," Claire lied. "I get it."

"Then Amelia came along." His lips pricked into a smile. "She's been a handful since day one. She reminds me of you, actually."

"I don't recall ever shoplifting."

"Don't you?" Ryan arched a brow. "You were always nicking chocolate from the post office because your mum wouldn't buy it for you."

The memory dragged itself from the depths of Claire's brain; how could she have forgotten? She almost felt embarrassed at how she'd demanded the chocolate back like a bossy adult who had somehow forgotten she'd ever been a child.

"Then Hugo came a few years later," he continued, finger tracing a stained ring on the table. "He's a little mini-me. Just as quiet as I was. He's a sensitive little kid. I don't know how they're going to get through this. Their mum just left."

Like you left me, Claire thought.

"She didn't even say goodbye," he continued. "She packed a bag, left me a letter, and went. The letter said she'd been having an affair with Will for five years. She wasn't happy. Felt trapped. Needed a fresh start. She was sorry. That was that."

"Wow."

"Yeah." He forced a dry laugh. "I didn't know what to do. Spain didn't feel like home anymore. I tried to make it work, but everything fell apart. So, I returned to the only other place I'd ever called home. Northash called me back, and there's no better place to raise kids. I just wish we were here under different circumstances."

"Are you glad to be back, though?"

"Honestly?" He smiled. "I am. I didn't realise how much I'd missed the old place. All the faces are the same, just older. Nobody recognises me, of course, so I get a fresh start too. The kids seem to be settling too. Got them into Northash Primary School. They start after the Easter holidays are over. I'm trying to find us a house, but trying to rent in Northash is like finding a needle in a haystack. Everything is for sale, and I'm living hand to mouth at the moment. The B&B is cheap, but not that cheap."

Claire almost felt guilty for her self-pity party. She had spent the past few weeks feeling like she had it hard, and yet she had a roof over her head and a family to support her. Ryan had no one in Northash to take him in, and he had two young children to think about. She wanted to apologise, even though she hadn't created his situation.

"I'm glad you're back," Claire said, meaning it. "I missed you too."

"It's just like old times, isn't it?" He slapped her on the knee. "See any of the old gang from school?"

"Just Sally." She looked down at his hand; it only lingered on her knee for a split second. "She's an estate agent. Married with two kids. Little demons, if you ask me."

"How old?"

"Thirty-five."

"I meant the kids." He laughed.

"Oh." She joined his laughter. "Four, I think. Maybe five?"

"And two girls?" He sucked the air through his teeth. "Wouldn't wish that on my worst enemy."

Claire's phone pinged in her handbag. She pulled it out, knowing exactly what it was when she saw it was a video from Damon. She flipped her phone over and pressed play.

"What's that?" Ryan asked, glancing over her shoulder. "Looks like an old episode of *Big Brother*."

"Camera from the work toilets," she explained,

squinting at the bathroom stall doors. "If this is what I think it is, it clears Belinda."

"The woman on the news?"

"I work with her."

Claire scrubbed along the five-minute video with her finger, cutting to the end. There was no sound, but when the middle bathroom stall opened and she saw Belinda's shocked face, cigarette hanging from her lip, she knew what Belinda had just heard; Nicola's fall.

She exited from the clip to read Damon's message:

Already sent to the police with the timestamps. Proves Belinda couldn't have done it. You were right!

"Is that the same Damon from school?" Ryan asked casually, sipping his beer. "Never knew you two were friends."

"We became friends. He works at the factory."

"Always a bit weird, wasn't he?" Ryan chuckled. "A proper sci-fi geek, if I remember correctly."

"He prefers nerd," Claire found herself saying, the defensiveness for her friend rising up. "He's really nice. He's been there for me a lot."

Claire hadn't meant to put the subtext 'and you haven't' out there, but she had, and she knew Ryan had picked up on it.

"Is Damon your boyfriend?" Ryan asked after another sip.

"I told you I was single."

"You told me you weren't married."

"Well, he's just a friend," she explained, slotting her phone away. "Haven't had a boyfriend as such."

"Ever?"

"No." Embarrassment made her guts twist. "I've tried the whole 'dating' thing, but it never seems to stick. I've never met a man who I gel with like—"

"Like?"

"Doesn't matter." Claire finished her pint, glancing at the clock. "Right, I should probably get going."

"And I need to get to work." Ryan drained his pint. "Let's do this again, yeah?"

"I'd like that."

"Maybe not before I start work, though." He ran his hands down his pale cheeks, his fingertips leaving red blush streaks. "That's gone right to my head, and I have back to back training sessions till lunch."

After finally exchanging numbers and promising to add each other on Facebook, they parted ways. Claire lingered outside the pub until he walked through the gym doors. She couldn't say if she still loved Ryan, but she was glad to have him back in her life.

But her thoughts didn't linger on him. They went straight to the murders. She'd left home feeling more defeated than ever, but knowing she was right about Belinda being innocent had renewed her self-confidence.

Looking ahead at the empty shop, she accepted it

wouldn't become her candle shop. The dream was dead for now, but at least she could solve the murders.

She was close.

Too close to give up now.

As though the universe wanted to send her a message, Graham walked out of the post office, suited and booted, carrying a briefcase. He looked a far cry from the meek neighbour she'd seen the other night; he now looked like a shorter, scrawnier version of his late wife.

Graham glanced around the square as he walked back to his car, and his eyes met Claire's. They lingered for a brief moment before he ducked into the car, as though he hadn't seen her. Even from a distance, she was sure she had caught his jaw clench.

Attempted kiss or not, at that moment, she knew Graham had another reason for wanting her as far out of the picture as possible. With Belinda out of the frame and the police's apparent disinterest in Ben, the finger now pointed at one person. Come rain or shine, Claire was going to try her hardest to prove her suspicions.

$\mathcal{C}$laire spent the rest of Thursday theorising with her father at the bottom of the garden. Using paper pilfered from her mother's printer, which she only ever used to print off recipes, and string from her sewing kit, they put together an investigation board on the shed wall. When every detail was laid out in front of them, they stood back and saw what Claire had expected – most of the strings stemmed from and looped back to Graham.

Claire awoke early the next morning, Good Friday, on purpose. By the time her mother knocked on the door with a cup of coffee, Claire had already made a fresh batch of small vanilla candle tealights.

"I think I'm close," she said, offering one to her mother to sniff. "They need to set and cure before I can light them to see, but I think I'm getting there. Might not need that missing page of my black book after all."

"Very nice, dear," she commented, barely sniffing it. "You know it's Nicola's funeral today?"

Claire jumped in the shower almost immediately. Considering the fuss the *Northash Observer* had made over Nicola's death and the subsequent shoddy investigation, she couldn't believe word of the funeral hadn't spread around the village faster.

"You shouldn't go," her mother said, following Claire, dressed all in black, to the front door. "You weren't invited, and the paper said it was a private funeral. Please, Claire. Don't make a scene."

Claire left the cottage alone, unsure of her intentions. She didn't know she'd had such a keen interest in going to the funeral until she heard about it. By the time she had dried off after the shower, she knew she needed to be there.

She'd seen Nicola die.

She couldn't undo that.

Trinity Community Church sat on the flat corner of Warton Lane before it sloped up under The Canopies and up to the factory. Apt, Claire thought, that Nicola's final resting place should be on a lane named after her great-great-great-grandfather. Cars lined the narrow lane on either side, blocking the road. Past the shady trees lining the church, she saw a sizeable group of attendees already gathered around a fresh plot in the small graveyard.

She was too late for the service, but during her walk from the cul-de-sac to the church, she'd decided she wouldn't go in anyway. Like her mother had said, it was a private ceremony, and she wasn't about to confront Graham at his wife's funeral.

Instead, she stood on the other side of the street under the shade of the trees and leaned against the high wall. It didn't take long to realise she wasn't the only one. She spotted Belinda staring ahead, hidden away behind an old green lamppost.

Claire didn't hesitate to join her.

"They almost charged me with her murder," Belinda said, smiling meekly at Claire. "Answering my phone to you clued them in on my location. Who knew phones worked like that?"

"I didn't set you up."

"I know." Belinda sighed. "You did much more than that. You saved me. If it weren't for that video, they thought they had enough to charge me. But then the chewing gum DNA came back, and it strengthened my case."

"DNA?"

"They found nicotine gum at the scene," Belinda explained, and Claire played along like she didn't know. "Took swabs from me and everything. Not that it mattered in the end. The DNA on the gum was from a man, and it doesn't match anyone in their records."

"Oh." Claire was surprised she hadn't heard that the DNA was male-specific. "I'm sorry for not telling you about what happened."

"I've had a lot of time to think." Belinda patted Claire on the arm. "I would have done the same. Losing Jeff has put everything into perspective. I lost him a long time ago, but knowing I'll never talk to him again..." She trailed off and gulped, obviously fighting tears. "How do I live with that, Claire?"

"One day at a time."

"I don't know how I'll be able to go back to work." She patted her pockets until she found her box of cigarettes. "Everyone will have been talking about it. They put my face on the news."

"People have short memories around here."

"At least I'll have you there." Belinda pulled the last cigarette from the packet and gazed at it. "I keep saying I'm going to quit. Every final cigarette of every packet is my last one, until the next packet. Maybe whoever killed Jeff was onto the right idea with that nicotine gum?" She laughed dryly, but it quickly turned to tears. "Who would want to murder him, Claire? I wanted to murder him after what I found out, but I never got the chance."

"Someone in your position," Claire said, staring ahead

at the black-coated mourners around the graveyard. "Someone more ruthless, with much more to gain."

"Who?"

"Our new boss," Claire said, catching herself. "Or should I say *your* new boss. As of yesterday morning, I am gainfully unemployed."

"What?" Belinda choked on the smoke. "You finally quit?"

"Fired." It was Claire's turn to laugh. "Graham reported me to the police. Remember when I took that bag of equipment ready for the bin?"

"You're kidding!"

"I wish I were."

"Who grassed you up to Graham in the first place?" Belinda asked. "It was going to be thrown out anyway."

She had been too preoccupied with why Graham had gone straight to the police that she hadn't given a second thought to how he'd even found out she'd taken the stuff.

"Maybe Nicola knew and had a record?" she thought aloud. "But surely she would have just fired me herself. She was desperate to cut back on costs."

As though aware she was being talked about, Nicola's coffin began to lower at a snail's pace compared to the descent that killed her. Neither spoke until it vanished below ground level. When they finally looked away, they weren't alone.

"Oh, hello again," Belinda said, nodding at Ben

Warton as he walked down the lane towards them. "If you're here for your sister's funeral, you just missed it."

"Did you see the witch go into the ground?" he asked, leaning against the wall on Belinda's other side.

"Yep."

"Then that's good enough for me."

The three of them stood in silence, staring ahead as the funeral party tossed handfuls of dirt onto the coffin. Claire felt like she had missed something important; she had no idea Belinda and Ben even knew each other.

"He was at the station when they released me," Belinda whispered to Claire when she seemed to notice her puzzlement. "Gave me a quid to get a coffee. He's all right."

"You work at the factory," Ben stated, nodding at Claire. "I suppose I should apologise."

"What for?"

"For messing with you." His usual smirk softened to something more human. "According to my latest therapy session, I've been too fixated on settling old scores. She said running the factory into the ground probably wasn't the best way to cope with everything that happened. I spent too many years in prison thinking about destroying that place; I just never thought I'd do it from the inside. Might have got away with it if not for Graham lawyering up. Didn't think the idiot had it in him."

"Why did you want to run the factory into the

ground?" Claire asked, unable to believe she was talking face to face with Ben after watching his strange behaviour from afar.

"For fun." He shrugged. "To get my own back. When my therapist pointed out the two people I wanted to get revenge on were already dead, she made me realise I'd already won. I suffered in prison for years. Kept my nose clean and behaved myself, which isn't as easy as they make it sound, believe me. There's more crime happening behind bars than out here. I lost every appeal until the one after my father died. I guess Nicola did me a favour finally bumping the old idiot off."

"He thinks Nicola killed William Warton," Belinda whispered to Claire, as though she'd already heard the story and didn't believe it.

"I don't *think*," he said, leaning forward to make eye contact with each of them in turn, "I *know*. Why is nobody suspicious of the fact that my father died the same way I supposedly attempted to murder him all those years ago? Heart attack? Come on. My father was a fit and healthy man. Didn't smoke, didn't drink, and ran marathons twice a year into his sixties. You two must have seen him up until the end."

Belinda and Claire glanced at each other. They'd had a similar conversation between them, commenting on how William had looked so well. Everyone had remarked on the cruelty and brevity of life. Any of them could go at any minute, they'd all said. Like with Bilal's death, people quickly forgot the details.

"Nicola framed me back then, and the witch got away with it." He glared around at the church. "She was always hell-bent on getting her hands on that factory, but she was too much of a daddy's girl for my father to see it. He died thinking I'd tried to kill him, and I have to live with that, but I swear on my mother and father's graves that I didn't. I did some terrible stuff. I stole from him, I lied to him, and I messed up more times than I'd care to admit, but I never tried to kill the man." He frowned. "Not that I can prove it now. The only person who could corroborate my story was just lowered into the Warton family plot – which I'm no longer allowed to be buried in, thanks to my father's will. I don't say this lightly, but I hope the witch rots in hell." He kicked away from the wall and stuffed his hands into his pockets. "I always thought Graham had more decency in his little toe than I have in my whole body, but the more I think about it, the more I realise nobody who could spend that many years with my sister could have any goodness left in them. If I were you, I'd get as far away from the factory as you can."

"I've already been fired," Claire admitted.

"Then he's done you a favour." He winked. "As for me, I'm off. I don't know where, and I honestly don't care. Anywhere but here. He's welcome to the factory. I came up to say goodbye to the place. Goodbye to my father, I suppose. That factory ran through his veins, and I thought it would mine one day, but my dear sister made sure that would never happen. As far as I'm concerned, the place is cursed. My father, Nicola, that boy falling into the vats. If the place wasn't haunted before, it is now. I'd say I'll see you around, but I won't."

Ben popped up the collar on his black coat and set off down the lane. The funeral party made their way to the gates. Graham was amongst them, unsmiling but dry-eyed. He could have seen them if he looked up, but he jumped straight into one of the black cars before anyone could stop to talk to him.

"Did you believe any of that?" Belinda asked as they walked away from the church. "About Nicola framing him and killing their father?"

"I'm not sure," Claire confessed, her mind spinning with the possibilities. "He seemed convinced. I don't think he was lying."

"Neither do I. When I spoke to him at the station, he said he was there to tell them he wasn't going to be around. They kept dragging him in for questions, but they had even less on him than they had on me and he had solid alibis for both, or so he says. Camera footage of him drinking in a bar outside the village. And the chewing gum DNA didn't match him. He doesn't even smoke."

They parted ways at the bottom of the lane. As Claire

walked home, she accepted that she had believed every word Ben had said. Perhaps he was an excellent liar and she was a gullible fool, but his words had felt honest.

"Your father and Uncle Pat are in the shed," Janet said with a roll of her eyes when Claire joined her in the kitchen. "They're playing *Cluedo* again with this case. If you're going to join them, take this tray of tea."

Claire did as she was told, overhearing their louder than usual voices from halfway down the garden path. When she reached the shed door, they were arguing. She knocked with her foot and waited for her father to open up.

"What's all the noise?" she asked, setting the tray of tea and biscuits down on the cluttered workbench.

"*This!*" Pat cried, shaking the sheet of paper with Abdul's name and motive written on it, his cry so deep he had to pause to cough. "Your father won't let this go. I don't know how many times I have to say that Abdul had nothing to do with any of this, but I'll say it again for effect. Abdul had *nothing* to do with it!"

"It's *only* a theory," Alan snatched the paper from Pat and stuck it back on the shed wall with a drawing pin. "We can't cross out any lines of enquiry until they're fully confirmed. I know he's your friend, but it's staying up there."

"Hasn't the poor man been through enough, losing his son?"

"I never said that but—"

"You're *retired*!" Pat cried, ripping the paper down and tearing it in two. "This isn't a game, Alan."

"If I'm retired, why does it matter so much?" Alan pulled out a fresh sheet of paper, wrote 'Abdul – Bilal. Suicide/covered-up accident' on it, and stuck it back on the wall. "*My* shed, *my* rules! It stays up, or you get out."

"You're acting like boys," Claire said from her upturned plant pot in the corner. "The bickering isn't going to get us anywhere, and besides, don't you want to know what I've just found out?"

They both calmed down enough to sit and listen to Claire relay everything Ben had just told her. Her father scribbled down notes the whole time before sticking them up on the wall.

"I wouldn't put it past her," Pat said, his voice calmer now. "It lines up with Abdul's theory about Bilal."

"I thought you didn't believe that?" Alan pointed out, hobbling back to his chair to stare at the wall. "But you're right, it does. I'm not sure how it connects, though. If someone knew Nicola killed her father and used that as a motive to murder her, why Jeff?"

"Graham," Claire said again, sitting bolt upright. "It links back to Graham. He told me he liked William Warton. Called him the only father he ever had. If he knew his wife murdered her father, and then found out she was having an affair, surely that's enough to push him over the edge to – Well, to push her!"

"That makes sense," Pat said, nodding slowly, his finger tapping against his chin. "But the police don't even seem to be looking at Graham. There must be a way to catch him out before he sells the factory."

"He told you about that?" Claire asked.

"That's what the meeting was about," he replied, sighing heavily. "You might not be the only one out of a job by the end of the week. He wanted to warn us in case he couldn't pull things together, but I'm not sure how honest he was being. His mind seemed to be made up. We need a way to disprove his alibis, or all of this was for nothing."

"Alibis?" Claire asked, not realising he had any.

"I met with DI Ramsbottom this morning to ask if Graham was on his radar," her father explained. "At home both times, and apparently with a witness to back it up."

"Who?"

"Wouldn't say," Alan said, clearly frustrated. "But whoever it was, it seems to be enough for them."

"He must have paid someone to lie for him," Claire thought aloud. "How can we prove he wasn't at home? There must be a way."

They contemplated it for a considerable amount of time but came to no conclusions. When they finally left the shed, cups of tea drained, Alan and Pat seemed to be in better spirits with each other and parted on a handshake.

After eating some lunch, Claire locked herself in her bedroom to continue work on her vanilla candle formula. Writing in her little black book, an idea popped into her head. The more she tried to push it away, the deeper it burrowed, growing so unbearable that she had to pick up her phone.

"Damon," she whispered into her handset, peeking through her curtains and into Graham's garden on the other side of the fence. "How do you feel about breaking and entering again?"

CHAPTER FOURTEEN

"Qou were fine earlier," Claire's mother said, a hand on Claire's forehead. "You are a bit warm."

"It hit me like a ton of bricks a couple of hours ago." Claire coughed before pulling the covers more tightly up to her chin. "If you really want me to, I can come?"

"No, no!" Janet backed away, holding up both hands. Claire almost felt guilty for playing into her mother's constant fear of catching the common cold. "If you're ill, it's best you stay there. Don't want to be passing it onto the whole family, do you? I'd offer to bring you some leftovers, but you know your grandmother can't cook. Considering how insistent Greta was about us coming tonight, I wouldn't be surprised if she wants to poison us all. I wouldn't put it past her."

"Play nice." Claire coughed again. "Honestly, I'll be fine. I've got Sid and Domino to keep me company."

"Hmmm." She peered down at the cats, who were curled up on either side of Claire's head. She looked as though she was about to attempt to stroke Sid, but he hissed before she could get closer. "See! They're evil little things."

"They can sense evil."

"What does that mean?"

"Nothing." Claire fluttered her lashes as though she were about to pass out. "I'm not thinking clearly. Go. I'll be fine."

Janet lingered for a moment longer before backing out of the room, leaving Claire with the cats. She listened to her mother walk downstairs, followed by her father's clumsier footsteps. The front door slammed. Claire tossed back the covers and jumped out of bed, fully clothed and perfectly well.

"I thought she was never going to leave!" Damon cried, bursting out of the built-in wardrobe. "I almost suffocated in there."

"There's breathing holes."

"Stranger things have happened," he replied. "In fact, in an episode of *Doctor Who*, the—"

"*Damon!*" Claire held her hand up. "Another, yeah? We have a plan to stick to, remember? It's gone off without a hitch so far, so let's ride that wave of luck."

"I can't believe your gran just agreed to ask everyone round for dinner."

"I told her I'd explain later," Claire said, hurrying over to the window to look at Graham's back garden again. "Right, by the looks of the lights, Graham is still at home. My parents will be at Granny Greta's for at least two hours. I told her to drag out the courses as long as possible, and for the sake of messing with my mother, she seemed all too happy to oblige."

"Your family is weird," Damon said, joining her at the window. "Everyone in my family actually does hate each other, but you all seem to have this weird love-hate thing going on."

"It's all love."

"Even your mum and gran?"

"Deep down. Very deep down." Claire closed the curtains and quickly fed the cats their dinner. "Okay, since Graham is home and his car is still out front, we need to go to Plan B."

"Wait, what was Plan A?"

"We wait for him to go out so we can sneak inside using this." Claire pulled a silver key from her pocket. "It's their backdoor key. They gave it to us so we could water their plants when they went on a month-long cruise a few years ago. It was Mrs Beaton or us. I think they must have forgotten because they never asked for it back. So, technically, it's not breaking and entering, just—"

"Entering?"

"Exactly."

"I'm noticing a pattern of behaviour here." Damon scratched at the side of his head. "It's like you've been taken over by a brainwashing alien obsessed with skating impossibly close to the law."

"Now that does sound like a *Doctor Who* episode."

"Actually, it reminds me of—"

"*Plan B*!" Claire clapped her hands together. "I have an idea to get Graham out of the house, and you're not going to like it."

"Have I liked any of this so far?" Damon perched on the edge of Claire's bed. "Go on. Lay it on me."

Claire sat next to him and gathered her thoughts as she watched the cats finish wolfing down their dinner. Even though she hadn't eaten yet, it was one of the rare occasions she couldn't have eaten even if she tried; adrenaline coursed through her body.

"We need a way to get him out of the house, don't we?" she started. "So, I was thinking, one of us could call the police and tell them we saw someone breaking into the factory."

"Oh, dear."

"Hear me out!"

"Do I have a choice?"

"You could leave, and I'll do this on my own."

Claire waited, but Damon didn't reply. He exhaled

and nodded for her to continue.

"The police are likely to contact Graham since he now owns the factory," she continued. "He'll rush out, and even if he drives quickly, we'll still have a good fifteen minutes to have a look around."

"And what are we even looking for?"

"Anything." Claire pushed up her glasses. "I don't know exactly. A signed confession if we're lucky."

"And if we're not lucky?"

"Some documents." Claire stood up and began pacing. "Nicola had an office, and from the sounds of it, Graham never went in there. If Nicola really did kill her father, she might have something in there to prove it. And *that* could link back to Graham. If we can prove that he knew about it, it might be enough to show the police, so they don't think we're crazy."

"*I* think you're crazy!" Damon cried. "There's a lot of 'ifs' in there. You're suggesting we break into—"

"Let ourselves in with a key."

"You're suggesting we trespass," he corrected himself with a scowl, "in our boss's home on the night of his wife's funeral to try and prove that he killed said wife, and then Jeff, all based on what? A hunch and some unconfirmed male DNA on a piece of ciggie gum?"

"Something like that."

"You really are crazy. Utterly barking." Damon pulled his phone from his pocket. "If you hadn't been right about the secret camera and Belinda being innocent, I'd have already walked out. Luckily for you, and unluckily for me, I trust you more than I trust anyone else." He held the phone out and nodded at it. "Who's doing this?"

"You," she said, sitting back next to him. "I know too many people at the station. They might recognise my voice."

"They might recognise *my* voice!"

"So, put on a different one." Claire nodded at the phone. "And put 141 before you dial 999, so they can't see your number. Try to be quick and vague."

Damon did as he was told and dialled the number. Before Claire could decide to back out, the operator had put him through to the local police station.

"*Hello, dear!*" Damon cried, his voice high-pitched and somehow Scottish. "I was just drivin' oot and aboot near the candle factory, and I saw a huge group of ... erm ... yobos! Looked like they were breaking in, they did. Och, aye, you should make sure as they're not ... raving. Got to go, dear! Bye, now!"

Damon hung up and tossed the phone onto the floor, his face somehow even redder than a beetroot. The cats scattered and darted to the safety of under the bed. Claire and Damon silently stared at the phone, neither breathing.

"Well," Claire said finally after an eternity, "that couldn't have gone any worse."

"I panicked!"

"Oot and aboot?"

"I *panicked*!"

"Yobos?" Claire elbowed him. "Rave?"

"I told you, I panicked!"

"Why did you panic yourself Scottish?"

"Because you told me to put on a fake voice," he said, elbowing her in the ribs in retaliation, "and I went straight to Mrs Doubtfire!"

They stared at the phone again, this time for much longer. Neither moved until they heard a door slam. Claire bounced off her bed, ran downstairs, and peeked through the hallway curtain.

"I don't believe it!" She motioned for Damon to follow. "He's going out. I think it might have worked."

"There's no way that worked."

"No, I think it did." She held back the curtain enough for Damon to see Graham's car performing a clunky three-point turn in the cul-de-sac. "Thank you, Mrs Doubtfire!"

Leaving all the lights on in case her parents came home early, they snuck out the backdoor, and each helping the other, made it over the garden fence into Graham's. Unlike the perfect garden her father had spent decades cultivating, Graham's garden matched the inside décor: stark, bare, and the grass didn't feel real under her shoes.

"If this all goes wrong and Graham comes back," Damon whispered as Claire slotted the key into the kitchen door, "we could always go to Plan C."

"We don't have a Plan C."

"You're not the only one who can come up with plans, you know." Damon looked around as if he expected police helicopters to descend at any moment. "If Graham comes back, we threaten to blackmail him."

"Again, with the blackmail?"

Claire twisted the key, and the door opened.

"Again, with the trespassing?" Damon replied. "You don't get the moral high ground when you're the one holding the key."

"I have morals," Claire whispered, stepping into the brightly lit, stark kitchen, "but I also have nothing left to lose. The candle shop has gone. Well, I never had that, but it's definitely not happening any time soon. I've been fired from my job, and I have a police caution on my record. If Graham catches us, I'll snap myself into the cuffs. Besides, he *has* to have done it. All the strings point to him."

"What strings?"

"It doesn't matter," Claire called from the sitting room doorway. "We're clear. We don't have long. Start looking around. Paperwork, receipts, anything that links Graham to either murder. Keep an ear out for Graham's car, but he shouldn't even be at the factory yet."

"It's not too late to turn back."

"Turn back then." Claire was already onto the first step. "You trusted my hunch before, and this time I'm even surer."

Leaving Damon to dig around in the living room, Claire went straight to what would be her bedroom at home. She opened the door to Nicola's office, and the chill hit her immediately. The weather outside was pleasant, but this was the sort of chill that only settled into a room that hadn't been used for a while. She hurried over to the desk and sat in the chair. All of the drawers had locks on them, but after trying a couple, she concluded none were actually locked.

After five minutes of digging in the left side and finding nothing more than accountant paperwork, she moved onto the right, which had more of the same. The clock ticked louder with every passing second, and the illegality of what she was doing felt heavier with each tick.

"What am I doing?" she whispered to herself, leaning back and looking around the room. "I really have lost the plot. I'm talking to myself."

After checking everything on the desk, she moved onto the filing cabinets lining the walls, but they contained the same useless paperwork as the desk. There was a bookshelf with a couple of framed pictures: one showed Nicola in her cap and gown on graduation day, another was on her wedding day; her smile was bigger in the first picture.

She picked up the wedding picture and brought it closer. Graham had a full head of hair and was much thinner, and Nicola looked almost exactly as she had on the day of her death: pale with bloodred hair.

Claire wondered how long ago their wedding was. They looked like they were in their early twenties, which put it at least two decades ago. Had they loved each other then? She turned the frame over to find a date but found something else entirely.

It certainly wasn't what she had expected.

It was better.

Claire squinted at the tiny bag of pills taped to the back of the frame. The tape didn't look fresh, but it didn't look too aged, either. A couple of months old? Claire had skipped the drug experimentation section of her teenage years, but even she knew the tiny pills in the bag weren't the kind you could buy from a pharmacy.

The door hinges squeaked open. Claire turned, still looking at the pills.

"Damon, I think Ben was—"

It wasn't Damon.

It was the last person Claire would have ever expected to see in Graham's house.

"*Sally?*"

"*Claire?*"

The old friends stared at each other, the ex-candle factory worker holding a drug-concealing picture frame, and the estate agent wearing nothing more than a loose-fitting silk gown and brandishing a lamp like a weapon.

"What are *you* doing here?" Sally lowered the lamp and covered her body with her arms.

"I could ask *you* the same question!"

"I thought you were a burglar!" Sally stepped into the room, keeping her eyes fixed on the carpet. "This isn't what it looks like."

Claire arched a brow. "Isn't it?"

Sally sighed and nodded. "Actually, yes, it is."

"You're having an affair with Graham?"

"It's not as simple as that." Sally frowned, clearly not liking the judgement. "Why are you in Graham's house? He'll be back any second. He's just gone to—"

"Check on the factory," Claire butted in. "I know. I made that happen. Well, Mrs Doubtfire made it happen."

"What?"

Damon hurried upstairs, cutting off Claire's need to explain. Claire's friends looked at each other with the usual disdain they defaulted to whenever they were together.

"I thought I heard voices," Damon said, panting for breath. "What the hell is Sally doing here?"

"She's having an affair with Graham." Claire was

AGATHA FROST

unable to look away from her oldest school friend. "Sally
… I thought you were so happy."

"It's a long story."

"Then I suppose we need tea." Claire put the photo
frame with the pills attached back onto the shelf, unsure
of how it proved anything other than Nicola's possible
murder of her father or a casual drug habit that had yet
to rise to the surface. "I think my place would be better,
don't you?"

After dressing, Sally followed Claire and Damon
through the front door and across the grass connecting
the two cottages. She settled Sally at the kitchen table
with a cup of sugary tea before dragging Damon out to
the hallway.

"Would you mind waiting in the sitting room?" Claire
asked, biting her lip. "I think we need to talk woman to
woman."

"Whatever." Damon reached into his jacket and pulled
out a thick stack of envelopes. "I think I found
something."

Before Claire could ask about it, she heard her friend
crying in the kitchen. As important as the investigation
was, her relationship with Sally trumped everything else.
Perhaps they weren't as close as they'd once been, but
they had still experienced a lot together.

"Can it wait ten minutes?" Claire asked, glancing at
the envelopes.

"It's waited this long."

Damon walked into the sitting room and closed the door behind himself before Claire could ask what he meant. He turned the TV on loud enough to drown out Sally's crying, leaving Claire to join her at the kitchen table.

"I'm sorry," Sally whispered, wiping mascara streaks from her cheeks. "I don't know what you must think of me."

"Why are you apologising?" Claire grabbed her hand and squeezed hard. "You're like my sister, Sally. You can tell me everything, you know that."

Sally smiled through her tears, which only brought on more tears in the process. The look she gave Claire made her think Sally had forgotten somewhere along the way that she had a confidante. Claire would never burn that bridge.

"It's been going on for a few months," Sally began, using her sleeve to staunch her tears. "Paul left me, Claire. He's gone."

"*What?*"

"He packed a bag and left," Sally said, almost choking on the words. "Went to 'find himself,' whatever that means. Said we rushed into things and he needed space."

"But you have children."

"He video chats." Sally forced a laugh. "Men can do

that, can't they? They can up and leave. Mothers, not so much."

Claire decided against telling Sally the story Ryan had told her about his wife; she hadn't even told Sally he was back in Northash yet. Once upon a time, Sally would have been the first person she'd called after seeing Ryan. Sally was the only one who knew how Claire used to feel about him.

"Paul made his choice." Sally stiffened up. "It wasn't an affair. I know that's how it looks, but it's such a dirty word. Nobody was sneaking around."

"Graham was married."

"Yeah, in law." Sally sighed and looked around the kitchen as though searching for eavesdroppers. "Nicola and Graham's marriage had been a sham for a long time. They've been trying to get divorced for years, but they could never agree on terms. She wanted everything, and he wasn't willing to budge. So, they just stayed married. Kept up pretences for the public show of it. Nicola's father loved Graham. I don't think he would have accepted his daughter if she divorced. They were on shaky ground as it was, according to Graham. He was old fashioned like that, wasn't he?"

"He always talked about the family unit," Claire said with a nod.

"Well, they weren't a family." Sally glanced through the wall as though she could see the cottage next door.

"Nicola had been seeing Jeff for years, and Graham knew it. He was fine with it, or so he told me. Said it got Nicola off his case. This part is going to sound really bad."

"Go on."

"Nicola introduced me to Graham," Sally said, scrunching up her eyes. "I know it's weird, but I was in a low place. Paul had just gone, I was struggling with the girls, and then Nicola Warton offers to set me up on a date. I think she was doing it because she pitied Graham, but we ended up getting on. He's nice."

"I didn't know you knew Nicola."

"I didn't." Sally shook her head before sipping her hot tea. "Not really. We weren't friends or anything, but I was helping her look for buyers for the factory outside of official channels."

"You knew about that?"

"I've been trying to warn you for months!" Sally sank into the chair. "I've been dropping hints, telling you to get your dreams going. When you said you wanted to see the shop, I thought you'd found yourself a way out before it all went pear-shaped."

"I was fantasy shopping!"

"I didn't know that!" Sally's voice rose to match Claire's. "It's not my fault she wanted to sell. She was well within her rights. She seemed desperate to get the money so she could run off and start a new life abroad. Jeff was going to go with her. He had this wife. She sounded awful, had him trapped."

"Belinda." Claire clenched her jaw, knowing it wasn't Sally's fault she'd been spun a story. "She's not a bad woman, she's just a little lost. I work with her."

"Oh." Sally blushed. "Well, Graham was glad to be shot of Nicola anyway. But then she died, and things flipped upside down. Ben took over, and I had to help Graham find lawyers. I felt so bad sneaking around. Do you know how many times I wanted to come and knock on your door to see you?"

"Why didn't you?"

"Because you'd ask questions I wasn't ready to answer." Sally smiled sadly. "I didn't want to admit that my perfect little life had fallen down around me. We drifted apart because I was jealous of you."

"Of me?"

"You have the world at your feet!" Sally cried. "Nothing holding you down. You can do anything and go anywhere. That's what we were going to do. Graham and me, that is. Once he got the factory, Nicola's buyers finally came through with an offer. I told Graham to sell so we could be the ones to run off. I'd take the girls, of course, but if everyone else can get a new start under the sun, why can't I? Even Jane from the tearoom got out of Northash! Don't you ever just want to run away?"

"Never."

230

"Then you might be the only one." Sally sipped her tea. "This village feels like a fishbowl when things aren't working out. There are ghosts around every corner. You can't escape your past because it's always around you."

Claire understood what she meant, but she looked at it differently. The ghosts, even the bad ones, were just memories. And even when the ghosts came in human form, like Ryan, she would never wish them gone.

"That was you on the phone," Claire thought aloud, the pieces slotting together. "I was hiding under the bins at the factory, and I heard Graham on the phone with someone talking about money. He said he loved you."

"He does," Sally said quickly. "I love him too."

"Oh, Sally." Claire could barely look at her friend, but she had to tell her. "He tried to kiss me."

"He did what?"

"I didn't want it, and I certainly didn't reciprocate it," Claire explained. "But I was at his cottage last week looking for my little black book. Nicola stole it. It was in her office, and as I was leaving, he ducked in to kiss me."

"He wouldn't."

"He did." Claire grabbed Sally's hand. "I'm sorry, but you know I wouldn't lie to you. That's not all. He fired me."

"Because of the kiss?"

"I think so." Claire tilted her head side to side. "Partly,

at least. There's more, and you're definitely not going to like this. I think Graham killed Nicola, and then Jeff."

"What, no, he can't—"

"How well do you know him?" Claire jumped in, squeezing Sally's hand harder. "Don't you think it's odd he would want to sell so quickly after his wife's death, even if they weren't together? Before he kissed me, he cried in his kitchen about Nicola. I don't think he was as over their marriage as he led you to believe. I think he snuck into the factory and pushed—"

"No, you don't understand," Sally interrupted, letting go of Claire's hands. "He can't have killed Nicola or Jeff because he was with me. Both times. We were in his cottage. And I told the police as much."

"Are you lying to me right now?"

"I wouldn't," Sally said, frowning. "I haven't lied; I just haven't told you the truth."

Claire fell back into her chair, her entire understanding of the murders falling down around her like someone had just ripped all the strings from the investigation board in one swift motion.

"But I was so sure," Claire said, almost to herself. "Everything points to him."

"I promise you." Sally pulled her phone from her pocket and flicked through her pictures. "Here, look. I took this silly selfie of us the day Nicola was killed. Look at the timestamp. It's minutes before she was pushed. We were both next door, watching daytime TV."

Claire stared at the picture of their faces warped with artificial dog ears and giant red tongues. They almost looked like a cute couple.

"And when Jeff … Well, we stayed up all night watching films together," Sally said, slotting the phone away. "The police looked over the movie account and it confirmed we were both there. Well, it confirmed someone was there, but it was us. I promise you. Graham couldn't have killed either of them."

Dazed and confused, Claire left the kitchen and walked into the sitting room. The TV was still playing, but Damon was engrossed in one of the letters from the stack of envelopes he'd taken.

"Graham can't have killed either of them," Claire said, her brows so tightly wound she was sure they'd merge in the middle. "He was with Sally. I was wrong. I was so wrong. We're back to square one."

"No," Damon said, his eyes dark as he held out a letter to Claire. "I don't think we are."

"What is it?" Claire accepted the letter.

"The final letter in a string of about fifty threatening Nicola." Damon pulled off his glasses and leaned on his knees, his hands running over his face. "I'm so sorry, Claire. I think you should read it."

I won't warn you again. You were told about the safety of the railings several times. You were told about the safety of the exposed vats several times. I tried to stop this happening. You know what you're doing. You're cutting corners, and you're lying to everyone. Bilal fell into that vat because you didn't want to admit that the factory needed a serious cash investment to make it safe. I know you wrote that suicide note in Bilal's name. You won't get away with this.

This is your final warning.
Confess, or you know what happens next.

Claire's hands shook so furiously, the letter she held rustled louder than the episode of *EastEnders* on the TV. She scanned the letter again, unable to take the words in.

"It's not signed," Claire said, tossing the letter back. "Anyone could have sent it."

"But you recognise the handwriting, don't you?" Damon stood slowly, showing her the rest of the letters. "These were stuffed down the back of the shoe rack. Nicola wasn't taking them seriously, but he was very serious. You recognise the handwriting. You must, because I do. He's been writing our reports for years."

"I recognise it." Claire attempted to gulp, but her

mouth was as dry as a bone. "How could I have been so wrong? He's been at the centre of this whole thing, and I never saw it."

"Never saw what?" Sally asked, appearing behind her.

"Call Graham," Claire instructed. "I think he should be around to hear this."

CHAPTER FIFTEEN

*A*s difficult as it was for Claire to bite her tongue, she decided to wait until Graham arrived to fill them in on her theory. In the ten minutes it took for him to drive back into the cul-de-sac, Claire had a clearer idea of what had been going on.

"I'll go and meet him," Sally said, jumping up quickly. "He's going to be a little confused."

"So, are they an item?" Damon asked the second they were alone.

"Sort of."

"I thought Sally was happily married?"

"So did I." Claire stared at the letters on the table. "I suppose you never really know what's going on beneath the surface."

Graham's voice began to rise; Sally did a good job of

calming him down. The front door opened. Deciding she didn't want to be on the back foot, she met them in the hallway instead of waiting for them to come to her.

"You *hoaxed* the phone call?" Graham cried, shrugging off his jacket with heavy reluctance. "And then you *broke* into my house to try and prove I murdered my wife and her lover?"

"You did call the police on her and fire her, amongst other things," Sally said softly as she hung his jacket. "And she didn't break in, she had a key. The key you gave her parents when you went on that cruise with Nicola."

"But *murder*?"

"Her story was quite compelling." Sally went to rest her hand on his shoulder, but it didn't quite make contact; she scrunched up her fingers and pulled back. "If I hadn't been with you at both times, I might have believed it myself. Let's just listen to what she has to say."

"This had better be good."

Sally and Graham sat on either side of Damon on the sofa. Claire thought about taking her father's tatty old armchair, but she opted to stand. The adrenaline had yet to ebb. It didn't take long for the standing to turn to pacing.

"C'mon then!" Graham demanded. "How could you possibly think I murdered two people?"

"I got it wrong," Claire admitted, "and I'm sorry for that, but if I hadn't let myself into your cottage, I probably never would have found out Sally was your alibi, nor would we have found these letters."

Graham glanced at the letters on the table. He didn't go in for a closer look, making it obvious he already knew about them.

"They started turning up at the house after that poor lad fell into that vat of wax," Graham explained, his tone softening. "No stamps, so they were clearly hand-delivered. They were on the doorstep every Tuesday when we woke up. I told Nicola to set up some cameras, but she didn't take the letters seriously. Said someone was probably trying to get something out of her. She wasn't going to crack; she was stubborn like that. I wanted to take them to the police. She wouldn't listen."

"She wasn't scared of them?" Sally asked, reaching forward to pick up one of the letters. "They might not be saying it openly, but it sounds like they were threatening to kill her. They really thought she covered up Bilal's death to make it look like a suicide."

"Did she?" Claire asked Graham directly.

Graham's lack of reaction gave a lot away. He leaned back into the sofa, one of his arms going around the back of Damon's head. The other rubbed as his forehead like he was trying to scrub away his thoughts.

"I don't know," Graham admitted, his tone soft. "I didn't want to think she could, but the way she denied it, it was always too much. As much as she didn't like to acknowledge it, I knew her better than anyone."

"That says a lot," Damon said, almost under his breath. "If she couldn't convince you, then she clearly did it."

"But why?" Sally asked, leaning forward to look across at Graham. "If Bilal's death was an accident, why would she go to the effort of faking a suicide note?"

"Because she was warned." Damon dug through the letters until he found a specific one. "Listen to this. 'A safety report was submitted to you two weeks before Bilal's fall, and the broken railing was in there. I know it wasn't fixed. I saw it with my own eyes the day before Bilal's death. Did you think you could get away with fixing the railing after and nobody would notice? I noticed. I know the truth.'" He put the letter back and picked up a second. "And this one says, 'You knew Bilal was on antidepressants. You gave him a warning for taking time off, so he told you the truth. You used that against him in his death. You're the sick one. You won't get away with this.'"

"She thought it would blow over." Graham waved his hand dismissively at the letters. "She thought they were silly. She'd laugh when another showed up. I think she enjoyed the drama of it. In fact, I remember her joking that the writer should have used letters cut from newspapers to really hammer home the clichés. It was all a joke to her."

"When was the final letter?" Claire asked, still pacing.

"The day before she died."

"And I assume you haven't had any similar ones since?"

Graham shook his head.

"But who wrote them, Claire?" Sally asked, edging forward. "You said you'd figured it out."

Headlights pierced through the night and shone through the curtains. Claire let out a steady stream of shaky air through her lips; it didn't slow the pounding of her heart.

"They're back," she said, turning to Damon. "I need you to do one more favour for me."

As Claire had expected, her parents had returned home with Uncle Pat and Granny Greta for their usual after-dinner whisky. Claire's mother was so stunned to find she already had a full house, she didn't seem to notice Claire's sudden recovery from her feigned illness.

"Don't disappear," she whispered to her mother in the kitchen as she retrieved as many glasses as she could for the extra guests. "This is one evening I don't think you're going to want to miss."

"What are you up to?" she hissed back. "Why is Graham here?"

"You'll see."

Claire watched as they all took their seats around the kitchen table, glad to see Damon wasn't among them. He walked in from the hallway seconds later, one hand deep in his pocket. He nodded at Claire, confirming he'd found exactly what she'd asked him to look for.

In this, Claire hated being right. The weight didn't lift like it should have. Instead, she felt as though she had strapped boulders to her chest and jumped into a deep lake.

Leaving her mother to put the glasses on a tray, Claire sat between Sally and Damon at the table. Her father locked eyes with her straight away, begging for an explanation; he never missed a trick. Claire wanted so badly to tell him everything, but his reaction stopped her. Things needed to play out. After all, outside of the letters, she had no concrete evidence.

"Well, isn't this nice," Greta announced, unscrewing the whisky as the glasses arrived. "The more, the merrier, right? We've got ourselves a little party here."

"What's the occasion?" Uncle Pat asked, grabbing a glass. "Not forgotten someone's birthday again, have I?"

"No occasion," Claire replied, taking the bottle from her gran once she had poured her drink.

Sally and Damon filled their glasses as high as Claire did. Graham only added a splash, and he never touched it. Needing the courage, Claire drank as much of it as she could in one go. It didn't get more pleasant with time. In fact, this time, it seemed to burn much more. After tonight, she vowed, she'd never touch the stuff again.

"Let's play a game," Claire announced, rising to her feet. "A little party game."

"A game?" Her mother barely hid her grimace behind her polite smile. "Claire, what's going on?"

"It's my birthday!" Damon announced.

"I thought you said there was no occasion?" Pat replied before sipping his whisky. "Not that we need an occasion to have a drink with family and friends."

Claire opened one of the drawers in the dining room cupboards, glad to find a stack of printer paper and a bag of multicoloured biro pens. She didn't have a concrete plan, but for the first time since Nicola's murder, it felt like fate was finally on her side.

"I didn't want to make a fuss," Damon said, continuing the lie; his birthday was in July. "Claire insisted I come, so I wouldn't spend it alone."

Claire quickly ripped a couple of sheets into eight sections.

"Well, happy birthday to you, lad." Pat lifted his glass in the air. "At least you weren't working today! Isn't that right, Graham?"

From the bag of pens, she picked out eight black pens.

"Huh?" Graham called.

She swapped one for a red.

Even better, she thought.

"The factory," Pat continued. "Nobody likes working on their birthday, do they? Thought any more about next week's schedule?"

"I'm sorting it out."

"People would really appreciate going back to William's old rota," said Pat. "I know it had its issues, but I'm sure we could make it work if we all put our heads together. No need to jump right into selling the place, is there?" Pat drank again. "Sorry, I've probably said too much. Was I supposed to keep that secret?"

"I did ask," Graham replied.

"Well, I already knew," Damon announced, forcing a laugh. "Claire told me."

"He asked me not to tell anyone either," Claire said, returning to her seat with the items, "but you fired me, didn't you, Graham?" She spread the paper around the table. "Don't worry, I'm not holding a grudge. I did steal some things headed for the tip, after all." She passed around the pens, purposefully positioning the red pen. "Right, just a bit of fun! An ice breaker, as it were."

"But we all know each other, dear," Granny Greta said, looking around the table. "Sort of."

"Play along, Gran," Claire said, forcing the biggest smile she could until her gran appeared to realise something was off. "Let's all write down something about ourselves. A funny story, a statement, a secret …

anything. We put them into a bowl, and then we take it in turns guessing who wrote the statement. Does that make sense?"

"There's no bowl," Damon pointed out.

Claire picked up the dish of potpourri from the centre of the table and tipped it upside down.

"*Claire!*" cried her mother.

"I'll clean it up after." Claire gave her a sharp 'go along with it' look. "Right, heads down and write something."

Despite a slight hesitation, everyone played along and began writing. Claire scribbled down her secret and was the first to put her folded paper in the bowl. One by one, the bowl filled up until all the lids were back on the pens. Claire picked up the dish, moved the paper around, and handed it to Damon to pluck one out.

"'I have no idea what's going on right now,'" he read aloud.

"That's mine!" Claire's mother announced.

"You're supposed to let us guess."

"But I really don't know what's going on right now."

"It's Damon's birthday." Claire shook up the bowl and passed it to her mother. "Why don't you go next?"

Lips pursed so tight they looked like they might seal shut for good, Janet plucked out the top paper. She unfolded it and read it over once.

"'I once met Prince Charles in an airport,'" she read

aloud, rolling her eyes. "I don't know how many times I've heard this one. Greta, that's yours."

"Don't roll your eyes at me!" Greta sipped her drink. "I *did* meet him at an airport, and he was a very nice gentleman."

"I don't think Prince Charles would have been going on a flight to Benidorm," Janet muttered, fiddling with the back of her diamond earring. "But you go ahead and keep telling people that story."

"It was Amsterdam," Greta said. "And I swear on my life, it was him."

"Hear that, God?" Janet called up to the ceiling. "Now's your chance."

"It's *true!*"

"My turn!" Claire called out. She plucked out the answer written in red and unfolded it; the handwriting was the exact same as the letters, as she'd known it would be. "'I've never seen a full game of football.'"

"Who's never seen a game of football?" Graham muttered, finally sipping his drink. "That's impossible."

"I already know who it is," Claire remarked, folding the paper up and pocketing it. "I recognised the handwriting. Uncle Pat, that's yours."

"And proud of it!" he called out. "Never grew up with it, did we, Mum?"

"Not my cup of tea," Greta replied, swishing her drink around. "Bunch of men chasing a ball around a field? *Boring!* Now, rugby, that's a *real* sport. Do I get a turn, dear?"

Claire held the bowl out to her gran. She read over the secret. From the pure shock alone, Claire knew what the paper said.

"'I know who murdered Nicola and Jeff,'" Greta said slowly, pausing to look around the table, "'and they're in this room.'"

"Okay, this has gone too far!" Janet stood up, snatching the dish from Claire. "I don't know what sick game you're playing, young lady, but it ends now. You get stranger by the day, and I know you didn't get that from me. That's all your father!"

"Should I still guess?" Greta asked, holding up the paper.

"You don't need to," Claire said. "I'll admit it, it's mine, and it's true."

"What?" Greta laughed, looking around the table. "Claire? Are you serious?"

"Deadly."

Claire glanced at her father, who had been silent since they sat down. His eyes were trained on Claire as he swirled the whisky in his glass. She knew him well enough to know he'd known what was going on from the moment they returned home. He looked across the table at the murderer; Claire heard the penny drop.

"This whisky has gone right through me," Pat said, standing up. "I'll be back in two."

When Pat left the kitchen, Claire patted Damon's leg under the table. He pressed what he'd found into her hand. She followed her uncle into the hallway, and exactly as she'd expected, found him riffling through his coat hanging from the wall.

"Looking for these?" Claire called out, holding up the crumpled box of cigarettes. "Terrible habit, you called it."

Pat spun around, his eyes going straight to the box of cigarettes. He looked as panicked as a deer in the headlights before forcing a shaky smile.

"You got me," he said with a chuckle, holding his hands out for the box. "The stress sent me back to them. I've been trying to quit."

"Oh, I know," Claire said, barely able to look her uncle in the eyes. "The nicotine gum proves that."

"I'm sorry?"

"The gum." Claire inhaled deeply. "The gum you spat out when you buried Jeff's body in the woods."

Gasps came from the kitchen, but Pat's face didn't falter from the same perplexed smile. He still had his hand out for the cigarette box; his fingers shook. Nicotine withdrawals? Or the same adrenaline now coursing through Claire's veins?

"Very funny," Pat said, dropping his hand. "C'mon, Claire. It's no time for games."

"It's not a game, Uncle." Claire pocketed the cigarettes and swapped them for the piece of paper. "Your handwriting isn't that remarkable. It could be anyone's really, but we get used to these things, don't we? Damon's right. How could I not recognise it from all the reports you've written at work, and that's not even including all the birthday cards and Christmas cards."

Pat's smile dropped, his mouth becoming a firm line.

"I don't know what you're—"

"You do."

Claire walked into the sitting room and picked up as many of the letters as she could hold. When she returned, the rest of the guests were stood in the kitchen hallway, all staring blankly at Pat, who was frozen by the coats.

"You wrote all these letters." She tossed them into the air, and by the time they finished fluttering to the ground, tears ran down her face. "You did it, Uncle Pat. You murdered them."

"*Claire!*" Pat boomed, a finger outstretched, his eyes mad and wide. "Stop this now. You don't know what you're saying."

"No, I do." Claire wiped away her tears, furious with herself for letting them fall in the first place. "It was you, Uncle Pat. It was you all along."

"Claire?" Granny Greta pushed through. "Why are you saying this?"

"Because it's true, Gran." She couldn't look at her gran

either. "I wish it weren't. I wish there was another explanation, but there isn't. I was so convinced Nicola's murder was connected to the affair, but it can't have been. Jeff is dead, Belinda has a solid alibi, and so does Graham."

"And Ben Warton?" Pat cried. "What about him? He hated his sister."

"He did." Claire nodded. "But he didn't do it, either. He didn't write all of these threatening letters. The letters you have yet to bother bending down to get a closer look at. Why would you need to? You know what they say. You knew about that railing. You warned her about it, and she never listened. And it turns out you were right. Bilal didn't kill himself, did he? You wanted us to think he did because you didn't want the scent drifting in this direction. You knew I'd never consider *you*, but you weren't going to let your friend, Abdul, take the blame, so you pushed us away. Every time we talked about this, you tried so hard to steer us in every other direction. Isn't that right, Dad?"

Claire turned to the spectators, but her father wasn't amongst them.

"Your best friend's son died," Claire continued, bowing her head, "and you wanted to get revenge. You hoped your letters would scare her into confessing, but you couldn't get any reaction from her, so you confronted her, and then you pushed her through that window."

"You killed my wife?" Graham stepped forward, his bottom lip wobbling. "It was *you*?"

"*Wife*?" Pat scoffed, every muscle in his body appearing to relax. "Don't make me laugh! You didn't love each other. You both thought you were convincing the world, but I saw the truth. It would have knocked William Warton sick knowing the truth about your pathetic marriage."

"It's true," Greta said, tears clouding her eyes, "isn't it? You're not denying it, son. I know you. I gave birth to you. You killed those two people, didn't you?"

Pat looked around the room, his eyes landing on Claire. His nostrils flared as he took a step back towards the door. He wasn't the Uncle Pat Claire had known and loved her whole life; she didn't recognise the man in front of her.

"Whose side are you on, Claire?" he hissed. "Nicola was going to sell the factory! I did you all a favour."

"It is true!" Greta cried, collapsing into Janet's arms. "My own son!"

"Yes, I did it!" Pat took another step back. "I confronted her, and she admitted it to my face. She admitted to writing the suicide note to save her own backside. She looked pleased with herself, too. I saw red, and I pushed her. Who knew that window was so flimsy?

Just another health and safety issue. Ironic, don't you think?"

"She was my *wife!*" Graham cried.

"And she didn't care one bit about you!" Pat switched his gaze. "You might have been pretending everything was fine with this sick arrangement of husband and wife swap, but I heard you sobbing that night at your cottage. I was delivering one of my letters after our usual Monday night dinner and whisky here, and you were talking with your bedroom window open, pretending you were fine and happy about everything going on. Then, she left to go meet up with him, and you cried like a pathetic baby. I did you a favour."

"And Jeff?" Claire asked. "He needed to die too?"

"He was there!" Pat took another step back, his body inches from the front door. "Hiding in the stationery cupboard. They must have heard me coming up the fire escape. I wanted to catch Nicola off-guard. I'd waited months to confront her, but I knew she wasn't going to confess, so I was going to get it out of her one way or another. I was willing to lose everything for the truth. Just like you now, Claire. I just wanted the truth! And not just for me, for Abdul! It was tearing him apart!"

"And you got it," Claire replied, looking him dead in the eyes, "but we're not the same right now. I don't know who you are."

"It's still me," he pleaded. "Uncle Pat."

"But why did you need to kill Jeff?"

"Because he heard the whole damn thing!" Pat continued. "He heard me confront Nicola, and he heard her confess. When he realised what had happened, he fled the same way I did. He took those fire escape stairs four at a time and ran for the hills. He knew how it'd look. They'd eventually find his DNA all over her lips. He couldn't tell the police what he'd heard because it'd out his affair to Belinda."

"If Jeff knew it was you, why didn't he go to the police?" Damon asked.

"Because he didn't know it was me," Pat said. "He didn't recognise my voice. Can't say I'm surprised. It's not like we ever had a conversation despite working together at the factory for so many years." He turned back to Claire. "When you said you saw Jeff kissing Nicola just before I pushed her, I knew he must have been there, so I went to see him. Found him waiting for a taxi outside Gary's Mechanics with all of his bags. I should have let him leave, but he recognised my voice right away. I did the only thing I could think of."

"The only thing?" Greta stepped forward, using the bannister for support. "I raised you better than this!"

"I panicked!" Tears filled Pat's eyes. "I was already in so deep, Mum. I didn't mean to kill Nicola, not really. I wanted to scare her, but I was just so angry. She was so dismissive of Bilal's life, and everyone was moving on so fast. Nobody cared anymore. She was going to get away with it unless I did something. I didn't want to lose everything. My job, my life, my family. Getting rid of Jeff was the only way to keep the secret. And he knew! He told me himself! He *knew* about the railing, and Nicola told him to ignore it. Told him to stop reporting it. I didn't even realise the gum fell out of my mouth."

"You were too busy trying to bury a body," Claire reminded him. "No wonder you did it so close to the edge. He was almost twice as tall as you."

"Please, Claire!" he begged, holding out both hands. "You have to understand. I was just trying to do the right thing. Things got out of hand. I'm not a cold-blooded killer! I would never hurt any of you."

"You got Claire fired," Graham said. "You were the one who told me about the stuff she had. You suggested I call the police. 'Teach her a lesson,' you said. I had no idea how close you were until tonight."

"I just wanted her to drop this!" Pat cried, his anger returning. "Like you, Mum, with the teaspoons. Marley just wanted to scare you to stop."

"This is not the same as teaspoons!" Greta screamed in a voice louder than any Claire had ever heard her use before. "You're sick, Patrick! Sick! Not only did you murder two people, but you had your niece fired too?"

"She was playing silly games with her father!" He scrunched up his face, hands either side of his head. "I had to scare you away, Claire. I thought losing your job would make you stop."

"And yet, it gave me the drive to keep pushing." Claire lowered her head, no energy left in her body. "Can someone call the police? I don't think I have the stomach to do it."

Pat spun around and dove for the door handle. He swung it open and ran for freedom, but he crashed into Alan, who had a cane in one hand, and a pair of handcuffs in the other. Pat fell backwards, losing his balance enough for Alan to attach one side of the handcuffs to his younger brother's wrist. He tightened the other side around the door handle.

"I knew he'd run," Claire's father said, sighing heavily as he limped into the hallway towards the house phone on the table. "If you don't mind, I'd like to be the one to make this call."

Pat thrashed and screamed against the door loud enough that the rest of the cul-de-sac came out to see what was going on, including Mrs Beaton and a small army of cats. They scattered when two cars police zoomed into the cul-de-sac.

"Can I just say something?" Janet called out as the officers dragged Pat towards a police car. "I *never* liked him!"

CHAPTER SIXTEEN

*C*laire made feeble attempts to sleep that night, but her eyes never stayed shut for more than a few minutes at a time. How could they? Every time she closed them, her childhood memories played against her eyelids like movies; Uncle Pat was in all of them.

Donkey rides on the beach in Blackpool.

Caravan holidays in Anglesey.

Soggy camping trips in the Lake District.

Until tonight, they'd been a normal family like anyone else's; Uncle Pat had taken that away. He was a murderer, and yet Claire couldn't shake those happy memories.

She tossed back the covers and climbed out of bed, finally giving up on the idea of sleep. Sid and Domino glanced up at her from the bottom of the bed, too comfy to move. If a fairy godmother popped up and offered to turn her into a cat, she'd take it in a heartbeat.

"Such an easy life," she whispered, stroking them.

After pulling her dressing gown over her pyjamas, she crept downstairs, not that she needed to creep; no one else was sleeping, either.

Granny Greta remained where Claire had left her in the sitting room, still surrounded by all the photo albums she'd dug out from the cupboards. She clutched a glossy photograph to her chest, the almost drained whisky bottle pulled tight against it. Without needing to look at it, Claire was sure the picture showed Pat as a child.

"He was such a sweet little boy," Greta had kept repeating all night. "Barely ever cried. Never caused me any trouble."

Greta gave her a weary smile. Claire smiled back, but she didn't venture inside. She knew that tonight, her gran wanted to be left to her thoughts.

Claire found her mother in the darkened kitchen, where the only light came from the dim under-cabinet spotlights. The contents of all the cupboards covered the island, and Janet knelt on the marble counter in her pyjamas, scrubbing the insides. Claire had last seen this behaviour on the night of Alan's tumour diagnosis.

Janet didn't spot her, so Claire crept through the backdoor, not wanting to interrupt her mother's ritual cleaning. This was Janet's way of getting her rage out –

everything chaotic had to be returned to order. The polite smiles and perfect outfits would return in the morning.

Even without the soft glow of the light coming from the shed at the bottom of the garden, Claire had known where she'd find her father.

She didn't bother to knock.

"Can't sleep either, little one?" he asked, quickly wiping away his tears as she slipped inside. "Too much excitement, eh?"

Claire perched on her usual plant pot. She went to glance at the investigation wall, but every sheet had been ripped down, and only the pins and hanging string hinted anything had ever been there.

"We got it so wrong, didn't we?" he said, following her gaze. "Well, I did. You figured it out. My own brother. Maybe I'm ready for the scrapheap, after all."

"You'll never be ready." She reached out and rested her hand on his knee. "I stumbled across it. I got lucky."

"It wasn't luck," he said, smiling sadly. "Credit where credit is due. You cracked this one on your own."

She looked at the framed photograph in his hand. Alan and Pat were stood in front of a Christmas tree in matching pyjamas, arms wrapped around each other. She knew the picture well; it had sat on the fireplace for as long as she could remember.

"Christmas 1966," he explained, handing over the

frame. "I was ten, he was six. Things were tight that year. I knew Mum and Dad couldn't afford both our Christmas lists, so I told them to just get Pat what he wanted because he was younger. When Christmas morning came around, he realised I barely had anything to open, so he split his toys with me."

Claire smiled down at the picture. She'd heard the story many times, but never before laced with such sadness and heartbreak.

"We'll be all right, won't we, Dad?"

"'Course we will."

Alan attempted to smile, but he couldn't muster one, not even for her. The tears broke free, harder and quicker than they had all night. Claire wrapped herself around him, having only seen him cry like this twice before: the night of his father's funeral and the night of his tumour diagnosis.

The crying went on for what felt like an age, but she didn't move until the final tear fell. He wouldn't cry in front of her about this again; she knew him well enough to know that.

"C'mon, Dad," she said, helping him up from his chair. "I think it's time for bed."

Two days later, the weather was bright and hot on

Easter Sunday.

Sat at her dressing table, Claire smelled her latest batch of vanilla candle samples. She still didn't have the exact formula, but it was close enough to the one she remembered. She had no wax left, barely any fragrance oils, and considering her recent change in employment status, she couldn't afford to keep chasing the perfection of the ripped-out page. Considering everything that had happened, she was ready to let the quest for the perfect vanilla candle go.

Perfection, after all, didn't exist.

The revelation of Uncle Pat's murder spree had proved her family was nowhere near perfect. Claire had never thought it was, despite how much her mother liked to present that image to the rest of the village.

Talk of the murderer with the Harris family name would continue for the foreseeable future, and they had all accepted it, even Claire's mother. Much to Claire's relief, her weight, lack of a husband, and childlessness hadn't come up all weekend.

Leaving her candle-making station, she joined Sid and Domino at the window. They were looking down on Claire's father, Alan, as he tried to get the flames of the barbeque going. They had held an annual Easter Sunday barbeque for as long as Claire could remember. She almost couldn't believe it was still going ahead – and was even more surprised to learn it was on her father's insistence, not her mother's.

"We have to carry on as normal," he had said on Saturday morning. "We aren't the ones being charged with murder."

Leaving the cats to continue watching him from the window, Claire joined her father in the garden. Her mother and Greta were at the kitchen table, and even though they weren't saying much, they weren't spitting their usual insults at each other, either.

"How's it going?" she asked, resting her head on Alan's shoulder.

"I'll get the flames going soon," he replied after kissing her on the top of her hair. "Don't you worry, we'll be eating by lunchtime."

"That's not what I meant."

"I know." He smiled. "And I appreciate you for asking, but we're all going to be okay. We'll get through this together like a family should."

Claire heard the undertone; in her father's eyes, Pat was no longer part of the family. She imagined Pat sat in a cell, charged with two counts of murder, waiting for his call to come from the Crown Court for sentencing. Despite knowing what he'd done, she still couldn't shake the image of her short, sweet, Uncle Pat.

Claire's phone beeped in her pocket.

"It's Sally," Claire said as she read over the message. "She wants to meet me in the square."

"I'll drive you," he said, already stepping back from the barbeque. "That needs some time to catch anyway."

Claire never argued when her father was trying to make himself useful; it meant too much to him. Leaving Janet and Greta to their awkward silence in the kitchen, separated by a full buffet spread, they left through the front door.

"I think someone wants to talk to you," her father said, nodding towards Graham's cottage. "I'll wait in the car."

Graham, who was pulling up weeds in his front garden, smiled at Claire awkwardly. She had avoided seeing him since the events of Friday night, but they were neighbours; they couldn't avoid each other forever, and someone had to address the giant elephant in the room.

"Lovely day for it," he said, standing and pulling off his gardening gloves. "The barbeque, I mean."

"You're invited," she said.

"Thank you." He smiled, and he looked like he meant it. "I'll think about it." He stared down at his gloves as he slapped them against the palm of his hand. "I owe you an apology, Claire. I should never have tried to kiss you."

"It's fine."

"No, it's not." He met her eyes. "You're too kind, but it's not fine. I know it's a cliché, but I was in a bad place.

I've been in a bad place for a long time. Long before Nicola's death."

"It's understandable."

"As much as I hate to admit it," he said, pausing to suck the air through his teeth, "your uncle was right. I pretended to be okay with everything that was going on in my marriage, but I wasn't. I knew it was over, but I couldn't let go. I was the one dragging my heels with the divorce. I hoped the woman I married would return one day, but I don't think she ever existed. Nicola really was as ruthless as everyone said. I always tried looking for more, but I don't think there was any. After hearing what she did to poor Bilal, I know exactly who she was now. At least the poor lad's father finally got the answers he always wanted. Now that everything's come out, Ben has told the police his suspicions about Nicola killing her father. He's been singing that same tune about her framing him for years, but I never believed him. Maybe he was right all along. I suppose there's no way to know now. Everyone who knows the truth is dead. Alas, I suppose we can only look to the future."

Claire thought about mentioning the pills taped to the back of the photo frame, but Graham would find them eventually. Even if Nicola had murdered her father, everyone who could confirm it was dead, and Graham had already been through enough.

"And what does the future hold for you?" Claire asked,

shielding her eyes from the bright sun as it broke through the clouds. "Have you figured out what you're doing with the factory?"

"I have." He bowed his head. "Your friend, Damon, was kind enough to tell everyone about my plans to sell. They kicked me right out of that group chat, so I started reaching out to people one by one. I heard everyone's stories. People really rely on that factory, more than I ever realised. The joys of growing up middle-class, right? You never know how bad things are at the bottom of the ladder. I can't let that factory become luxury apartments knowing how many lives it'd ruin. I couldn't sleep with myself at night. So, I'm staying, and I'm going to give it my best shot."

"That's amazing news."

"Can't say I'll make it work, but I can try my hardest, can't I?"

"That's all you can do," Claire said, smiling. "William would be proud."

He smiled, and for the first time in a long time, Claire saw her neighbour again. She had always thought of Graham as a simple, kind man, and she didn't think her assumptions had been too far from the truth. He'd been pushed into situations he didn't want to be in, and which didn't show his best side, but he wasn't a bad man.

"I've been keeping myself busy," he said, stepping back and looking down at the weeds he'd yet to pull up. "I'll let you get on. I might see you later at the barbeque if I feel up to it."

"I'm just off to see Sally," Claire explained, glancing at her father in the car; he was reading one of his mystery books, quite content. "How are things between the two of you?"

"Over," he replied, already kneeling back onto the grass. "I called things off on Saturday night. To be honest with you, I only agreed to that because I thought it might make Nicola jealous. Sally's a nice lady, but I'm not ready for a commitment right now. I leaned into it for comfort when Nicola died, and we both got carried away with visions of new lives. As appealing as a fresh start is, I'm not ready to give all of this up. Not just yet. And who knows, maybe one day I'll meet a woman who wants the same things out of life that I do. Until then, I'm going to have my hands full with the factory." He paused and smiled up at her. "Good luck with it all, Claire."

"You too."

Leaving him to his gardening, Claire joined her father in the car. As they drove away from the cul-de-sac, she peered at Graham through the rear-view mirror. He hadn't offered to let her come back to work at the factory. She hadn't expected him to, and she wasn't sure she wanted it anyway.

Too much had happened to go backwards.

They drove silently into the village, parking outside

the post office. Claire was surprised to see Sally atop a ladder outside Jane's Tearoom, taking down the 'TO LET' sign.

"Who's the lucky person that signed on the dotted line?" Claire called from the bottom of the ladder.

"You," Claire's father said when he caught up with her. "It's yours."

"What?"

"Claire, how long did you think you could keep this secret from me?" he asked, a pleased smile spreading ear to ear. "I saw you viewing this place at least twice. I had a feeling what you were up to, but it wasn't till Sally called me yesterday that I realised how much you really wanted to open your own candle shop."

"Sorry, mate," Sally said as she climbed down the ladder, the sign tucked under her arm. "I had to. You were going to let this slip away, and after everything you've been through, I couldn't let that happen."

"I don't understand." Claire stepped back and shook her head. "I can't afford this."

"Yes, you can." Her father rested his hand on her shoulder. "Check your bank."

With shaky fingers, Claire pulled her phone from her pocket and logged into her banking app. When she saw that £3000 had been transferred to her account, she almost dropped the phone.

"Dad, I can't take your money."

"It's not *my* money," he said, holding up a hand. "It's *yours*. I talked to Graham yesterday. Turns out, he found the ripped-out page of your book at the factory after all, and after some negotiating, he decided to buy the formula from you to use as the star product for the new and improved Warton Candle line."

"Why didn't he say anything?"

"Because I told him not to." He winked. "Wanted to surprise you. I hope you don't mind. I think he was going to use the formula regardless, so it's only fair you get something for it after putting in seventeen years at that place. Plus, I think he feels guilty for everything that happened with firing you. It's enough to pay the deposit and get things rolling."

"Dad, I—"

He cupped her face in his palms. "I know you wanted to do this on your own, and I admire that, but you can't live your life with your dream just out of reach. Not when we can help you. As much as I love having you back home with us, I know it's not where you want to be."

"Dad, I don't know what to say."

"Just promise you'll give it your best shot."

"I promise I will." Claire fought back the tears. "This is truly all I've ever wanted."

"Then there's no way it can fail." He pulled her into a tight hug. "I've always been proud of you, but the way you investigated and solved that made me so proud to call you my daughter. I've never seen you so determined and driven before. It was a side I loved seeing, and if you work at this only half as hard as you worked at uncovering what your uncle did, you've got this in the bag, little one. Now, I'll leave you two to talk. I'll be waiting in the car."

When he was back in the car, Clair grabbed hold of Sally and hugged her tighter than ever.

"Thank you," Claire whispered to her.

"You don't need to thank me," Sally whispered back. "It's the least I could do. I've been a terrible friend to you, Claire."

"Sally, it's—"

"No," Sally cut in, pulling away from the hug. "I have. I really have. I haven't been there for you, and I shut you out because I was embarrassed. I hate myself for admitting this, but I've always known you were jealous of me. I didn't want to shatter that. Knowing you wanted what I had kept me clinging on in a small way, hoping it would be what I wanted too."

Sally reached into her pocket and pulled out a silver chain. Claire knew what it was immediately.

"You found it," Claire said.

"I never lost it." Sally fingered the necklace charm in her palm. "Best friends forever, right? I mean it just as much now as I did then, and I promise that I'll never lock you out again. I love you, Claire."

"I love you too." They hugged again. "Graham told me he ended things."

"I let him think that." Sally chuckled, pocketing the necklace. "I was going to end things, but he started talking first. I think he needed to think it was his call more than I needed to."

"So, what happens now?"

"I called Paul." She looked down at her shoes. "I told him everything. I insisted he come back, if not for me, for the girls. He's on the plane as we speak."

"Do you think there's a chance between you?"

"I don't know."

"Do you want there to be?"

"I don't know that either."

"And that's okay." Claire smiled. "Despite what people like my mother say, it's not the be-all and end-all, right?"

"Right." Sally looked over her shoulder and into the empty shop. "How do you feel about one last viewing before we sign the paperwork at the office tomorrow?"

"Sounds like the perfect plan."

While Sally found the key on the cluttered chain, Claire turned and looked around the village square. Most of the shops were closed as usual on Sunday, but the beer garden in front of the pub was busier than ever.

In the sea of faces, a familiar one jumped out.

Ryan smiled and waved.

Claire smiled and waved back.

"Who's that?" Sally asked after unlocking the door. "He's cute."

"I'll tell you later." Claire turned to the shop. "You're never going to believe it."

Standing in the middle of the shop, just like she had during her previous viewing, Claire imagined the candle shop as clear as day around her. She closed her eyes and inhaled, the dozens of different scents already thick in her nostrils. It might not have been how she imagined the dream coming true, but for the first time in her life, it was finally close enough to reach out and touch.

"Have you thought of a shop name yet?" Sally asked.

"Not yet."

"How about Claire's Candles?" Sally suggested, joining Claire in looking out of the window. "It's simple, but I like it."

"Claire's Candles." Claire closed her eyes again, absorbing the name. "I like it too."

The road to opening the shop would be difficult, and the fight to make it work in the small village would be even harder, but Claire was ready for the challenge.

For the first time in her adult life, Claire Harris didn't feel stuck, which made the future a dizzyingly exciting place to be heading.

Thank you for reading!

DON'T FORGET TO RATE AND REVIEW ON AMAZON

There you have it! The first book in the Claire's Candles series, and the first of many, I hope!

But that's down to you! Reviews are more important than ever, so show your support for the series by rating and reviewing the book on Amazon! Reviews are **CRUCIAL** for the longevity of any series, and they're the best way to let authors know you want more! They help us reach more people! I appreciate any feedback, no matter how long or short. It's a great way of letting other cozy mystery fans know what you thought about the book.

Being an independent author means this is my livelihood, and *every review* really does make a **huge difference**. Reviews are the best way to support me so I can continue doing what I love, which is bringing you, the readers, more fun cozy adventures!

WANT TO BE KEPT UP TO DATE WITH AGATHA FROST RELEASES? *SIGN UP THE FREE NEWSLETTER BELOW!*

www.AgathaFrost.com

You can also follow **Agatha Frost** across social media. Search 'Agatha Frost' on:

Facebook
Twitter
Goodreads
Instagram

Printed in Great Britain
by Amazon